MRS. BOB CRATCHIT'S WILD CHRISTMAS BINGE

BY CHRISTOPHER DURANG

★

DRAMATISTS
PLAY SERVICE
INC.

MRS. BOB CRATCHIT'S WILD CHRISTMAS BINGE
Copyright © 2005, Christopher Durang

All Rights Reserved

MRS. BOB CRATCHIT'S WILD CHRISTMAS BINGE was commissioned by City Theatre (Tracy Brigden, Artistic Director; David Jobin, Managing Director; Kellee Van Aken, Artistic Associate) in Pittsburgh, Pennsylvania, premiering on November 7, 2002. It was directed by Tracy Brigden; the set design was by Jeff Cowie; the costume design was by Elizabeth Hope Clancy; the lighting design was by Rick Martin; the sound design was by Elizabeth Atkinson; the original music was by Michael Friedman (the lyrics were by Christopher Durang); the musical direction was by Douglas Levine; the musical staging was by Scott Wise; and the production stage manager was Patti Kelly. The cast was as follows:

THE GHOST OF CHRISTMAS PAST,
PRESENT and FUTURE .... January Murelli
EBENEZER SCROOGE .... Douglas Rees
MRS. BOB CRATCHIT .... Kristine Nielsen
BOB CRATCHIT .... Martin Giles
TINY TIM .... Darren E. Focareta
LITTLE NELL CRATCHIT .... Sheila McKenna
CRATCHIT CHILD 1 .... Lauren Rose Gigliotti
or Allison Hannon
CRATCHIT CHILD 2 .... Shane Jordan
or Matt Lang
GENTLEMEN COLLECTING FOR CHRISTMAS
(KENNETH LAY, JEFFREY SKILLING) .... Jeff Howell
Matthew Gaydos
JACOB MARLEY'S GHOST .... Larry John Meyers
YOUNG JACOB MARLEY .... Lauren Rose Gigliotti
or Allison Hannon
YOUNG EBENEZER .... Shane Jordan or Matt Lang
MR. FEZZIWIG .... Jeff Howell
MRS. FEZZIWIG .... Sheila McKenna
FEZZIWIG DAUGHTERS .... Darren E. Focareta
Elena Passarello
THE BEADLE .... Jeff Howell
THE BEADLE'S WIFE .... Sheila McKenna
EDVAR .... Matthew Gaydos
HEDWIG .... Elena Passarello

CHARACTERS
(in order of appearance)

Young Jacob Marley (child)

Young Ebenezer Scrooge (child)

The Ghost

Ebenezer Scrooge

Bob Cratchit

Tiny Tim

Mrs. Bob Cratchit

Child 1 (Cratchit Child)

Child 2 (Cratchit Child)

Gentleman 1

Gentleman 2

Jacob Marley

Mr. Fezziwig

Mrs. Fezziwig

The Beadle

The Beadle's Wife

Edvar

Hedvig

Little Nell

Bartender

George

A Child (Zuzu) (girl)

Clarence

The Nice Mrs. Cratchit

Lovely Irish Voice (woman)

Tess's Voice

Serena, a maid

Main Characters:
(not to be doubled)

1. GHOST — black woman

2. EBENEZER SCROOGE

3. BOB CRATCHIT

4. MRS. BOB CRATCHIT

5. TINY TIM — played by young, boyish adult (can also play a Fezziwig daughter)

Ensemble:

6. LITTLE NELL — female (can also play Mrs. Fezziwig, the Beadle's Wife)

7. GENTLEMAN 1 — male (can also play Mr. Fezziwig, the Beadle, Act Two Bartender)

8. GENTLEMAN 2 — male (can also play Edvar, George Bailey, Voice of Tess, Serena)

9. GHOST OF JACOB MARLEY — male (can also play Clarence, Act One Bartender)

10. THE NICE MRS. CRATCHIT — female (can also play Hedvig, Lovely Irish Voice)

Children:

11. YOUNG EBENEZER — boy, age 8 through 13, can also play Cratchit Child 2

12. YOUNG JACOB MARLEY — girl, age 8 through 13, can also play Cratchit Child 1, and the child Zuzu (you can have four separate children play the roles above if you wish — three boys for Ebenezer, Jacob, and Child 2; and one girl for Child 1 and Zuzu)

MRS. BOB CRATCHIT'S WILD CHRISTMAS BINGE

ACT ONE

Scene 1

Christmastime. Dickens look, 1840s. A street in London. Two young boys, dressed in coats, hats-and-scarves stand next to one another. One boy is singing.

BOY 1. *(Singing sweetly.)*
   HARK THE HERALD ANGELS SING,
   GLORY TO THE NEWBORN KING
BOY 2. *(Irritated, negative.)* Bah humbug! Bah humbug!
BOY 1.
   PEACE ON EARTH, AND MERCY MILD
BOY 2. Phooey! Christmas stinks! Kaplooey!
BOY 1.
   GOD AND SINNER RECONCILED
BOY 2. Bah humbug! Get me a good hamburger!
BOY 1. *(Continues with the song softly. Enter the Ghost — a striking, theatrical black woman. She addresses the audience.)*
GHOST. Even as a child, young Ebenezer displayed a pronounced antipathy toward Christmas. *(To Boy 2.)* Merry Christmas, Ebenezer.
YOUNG EBENEZER. Bah humbug! Give me some Christmas pudding. I want to put bugs in your hair! Bah humbug!
GHOST. *(To audience.)* In later centuries, we would probably identify Ebenezer's repeated saying of "Bah humbug" as a kind of seasonal Tourette's Syndrome. However, in 1843, when our story is set, we hadn't a clue what it meant — except he was a nasty little child.

YOUNG EBENEZER. Bah humbug! I hate Christmas!

GHOST. *(To audience.)* Hello. I am the Ghost of Christmas Past, Present and Yet To Come, including all media yet to be invented. If you get me on DVD you can click on Special Features, and see twenty-seven other hairdo choices I have. But we're in a live theatre presently, so you'll just have to accept my hair as it is.

YOUNG EBENEZER. I want to put bugs in your hair!

GHOST. Children are so difficult, aren't they? You should see them backstage. I'm so glad I'm a ghost and I don't have any children.

BOY 1. I like Christmas carols, but my friend Ebenezer is slowly convincing me to hate Christmas.

GHOST. This is young Jacob Marley. And he and Ebenezer will grow up to run a business together.

YOUNG EBENEZER. I want to be very wealthy.

YOUNG JACOB. Me too!

GHOST. Oh you kids. I'd like to take a strap to you. But all you politically correct types don't like that. A good spanking never hurt a child, unless it got out of control and killed him, in which case it did. But I don't want to kill these children, I just want to make them behave. *(Screams at the children.)* BEHAVE!!! AND HAVE A BETTER ATTITUDE ABOUT CHRISTMAS!

YOUNG EBENEZER. I hate Christmas. Bah humbug.

GHOST. You have Tourette's Syndrome. You need to learn to be seen and not heard. *(To audience.)* And now meet Ebenezer Scrooge, grown up. *(Enter old Ebenezer Scrooge. He is sour, grumpy, cranky.)* Hello there, Mr. Scrooge. Merry Christmas to you.

EBENEZER SCROOGE. Bah humbug! I'd like to put bugs in your hair!

GHOST. Really, how strange. What kind of bugs?

EBENEZER SCROOGE. Oh awful crawling kinds. Beetles. Spiders.

GHOST. Uh huh. Mr. Scrooge, I'd like you to meet your inner child.

EBENEZER SCROOGE. What?

GHOST. *(To Young Ebenezer.)* Say hello to your grown-up self, Ebenezer.

YOUNG EBENEZER. I hate you! *(Kicks him.)*

EBENEZER SCROOGE. And I hate you, you little creep! *(Big Ebenezer and Young Ebenezer struggle with one another. Young Jacob looks on, passively.)*

GHOST. *(To audience.)* What unpleasant people. I wonder if I'll be able to make them appreciate the true meaning of Christmas before the end of the evening? What do you think? How many of you don't care? Never mind, I don't want to know. I have a job to do, and I've got to do it. Okay, you two, break it up.

EBENEZER SCROOGE. You should be sent to the workhouse!

YOUNG EBENEZER. You should be sent to a nursing home!

GHOST. Isn't it sad? Isn't it poignant and ironic how much Mr. Scrooge's younger and older selves hate each other? *(To Young Ebenezer and Old Ebenezer.)* You're dealing with self-hatred, you two, and you don't even know it!

YOUNG JACOB. Why don't I have any lines?

GHOST. Why does the sun come up in the morning?

YOUNG JACOB. I don't know.

GHOST. Well, that's why you don't have any lines. Okay, enough of this scene. Let's move on to the next one. Ready, Mr. Scrooge?

EBENEZER SCROOGE. Shut up, I don't know you. I don't think there even are Negro people in 1840's London.

GHOST. I stand outside of time.

EBENEZER SCROOGE. Well good for you. I haven't time for this, I'm on my way to work.

GHOST. Merry Christmas.

EBENEZER SCROOGE. Bah! Humbug!

YOUNG EBENEZER. Bah! Humbug! *(Scrooge exits, followed by Young Ebenezer and Young Jacob.)*

GHOST. Luckily, you know, most people aren't like Mr. Scrooge here. They love Christmas as I do, and as I hope you do too. *(Music begins. The ghost looks around the stage in pleasant wonderment. Sings.)*

    LONDON IS A-BUZZ
    LONDON IS A-GLOW
    PEOPLE MILL ABOUT IN GROUPS
    THEY WANDER TO AND FRO

(London townspeople start to come in and gather. They mill about in groups; they wander. They point at things in the set. A wandering person may be selling toys. The children point at them. They're all very happy and interested in Christmas.)

    THEY COME ONSTAGE
    FROM LEFT AND RIGHT
    FROM UPSTAGE, DOWNSTAGE TOO

    THEY COME TO TOWN
    THEY POINT AT THINGS

THEY'VE GOT A LOT TO DO
CHORUS.
   WE'RE ALL SO EXCITED
   WE'RE HAPPY AND DELIGHTED
   THE FUN HAS BEEN IGNITED
   WE GRIN FROM EAR TO EAR
GHOST.
   AND WHY IS THAT, THE REASON IS QUITE CLEAR
   THAT CHRISTMAS, LOVELY CHRISTMASTIME IS NEAR

   IT'S NEARLY CHRISTMAS
   LOOK AT ALL THE SHOPS
   THE PIGS ARE EATING SLOPS
   IT'S NEARLY CHRISTMAS
   THE AIR IS CRISP AND COLD
   [THE] CHILDREN GOOD AS GOLD

   IT SORT OF WEIGHS A TON
   THIS FESTIVE CHRISTMAS FUN
   AND YET WE WOULDN'T HAVE IT ANY OTHER WAY!
GHOST and CHORUS.
   WE LOVE CHRISTMAS, WE LOVE CHRISTMAS,
      CHRISTMAS DAY
(The Cratchit family, who have been part of the above, have now milled about into a center place so they may be featured. It's Bob Cratchit, helping Tiny Tim on his crutch. And Mrs. Bob Cratchit is being warm and motherly to two of her other children, Child 1 [girl] and Child 2 [boy].)
   HERE ARE THE CRATCHITS
   BOB AND TINY TIM
   IT'S SWEET AND IT'S TOUCHING
   BOB WATCHES OVER HIM
   THIS IS ONLY A GLIMPSE
   SAD TO SAY, THE CHILD LIMPS
   IT'S NOT QUITE CLEAR IF THERE'S A CURE
   STILL TINY TIM, HIS HEART IS PURE
TINY TIM. Anything sad or bad I just ignore. I love Christmas.
BOB CRATCHIT. I know you do, Tiny Tim. And your mother and I love it too. Don't we, dear?
MRS. BOB CRATCHIT. *(Not realizing she was going to be asked to speak.)* Oh yes. What? We love Christmas very much. *(Slightly weak smile, she's a bit tired.)*

10

EVERYONE.
  IT'S NEARLY CHRISTMAS
  SUCH A JOYFUL NOISE
  [THE] CHILDREN PLAY WITH TOYS

  IT'S NEARLY CHRISTMAS
  SNOW IS IN THE AIR
  A PARTRIDGE AND A PEAR

  IT MELTS THE HEARTS OF CRANKS
  THEY LEARN THEY MUST GIVE THANKS
  IT'S A TIME TO LAUGH AND SING AND DANCE
      AND PLAY
  WE LOVE CHRISTMAS, WE LOVE CHRISTMAS,
      CHRISTMAS DAY

(Mr. Scrooge comes back onstage, still needing to get to work. He didn't mean to come back this route and is horrified to see everyone.)

A CHILD. Look — it's Mr. Scrooge!

EVERYONE. MERRY CHRISTMAS, MR. SCROOGE! *(Mr. Scrooge is horrified, and it makes him nauseous. He starts to need to vomit, covers his mouth with his hand, runs offstage.)*

EVERYONE. *(Disappointed in his response.)* Ahhhhhhhhhhh.

TINY TIM. Mr. Scrooge doesn't know how to celebrate Christmas, does he, Father?

BOB CRATCHIT. *(Laughs.)* Indeed he does not, Tiny Tim! *(Everyone smiles, delighted. Mrs. Bob Cratchit smiles also, but it seems a little strained.)*

TINY TIM. God bless us, everyone! *(Everyone looks even more delighted. Mrs. Bob Cratchit looks at him, slightly sick of him, but it's subtle. It's possible we might not notice. She's trying to be agreeable and to love Christmas, mostly. It's just that, like her clothes, her nerves are threadbare.)*

GHOST. And God bless you, Tiny Tim! *(Tiny Tim beams. In the following, done in a very musical comedy/*Oliver! *kind of way, Mrs. Bob Cratchit gamely moves with everyone else, but is a bit out of synch sometimes.)*

EVERYONE.
  IT'S NEARLY CHRISTMAS
  THE REINDEER AND THE SLEIGH
  LET NOTHING YOU DISMAY
  IT'S NEARLY CHRISTMAS

THE JINGLE BELLS DING DING
LET'S GO A-CAROLING

IT'S TIME CONSUMING, TRUE

MRS. BOB CRATCHIT.
(To audience.) Yes it is.

IT MAKES SOME PEOPLE BLUE

Well, a little.

AND YET WE WOULDN'T HAVE
IT ANY OTHER WAY!

Well I would! *(Laughs.)*

WE LOVE CHRISTMAS,

Did I turn the oven
off?

WE LOVE CHRISTMAS,

Ohh!!! — where are
the other children?
*(She joins the last
sung line:)*

WE LOVE CHRISTMAS,

CHRISTMAS DAY!   CHRISTMAS DAY!

(Townspeople all disperse, waving at each other or maybe the audience. Mrs. Bob Cratchit fiddles with Bob's long scarf, making sure he's warm. Then she leads Tiny Tim and the other two children off, while Bob goes off in the same direction Scrooge had exited. Set change starts.)

GHOST. Well I hope you enjoyed that. Sometimes I prefer to sing a Billie Holiday song, but "Tain't Nobody's Business If I Do" doesn't seem very Christmasy. So it's time to begin our journey of redeeming Mr. Ebenezer Scrooge. And the first place we should go is his place of work, the office of Scrooge and Marley. Because Mr. Scrooge felt sick to his stomach, luckily Bob Cratchit was able to get there first. *(Seeing the set is complete:)* Ah, and here's the set change.

Scene 2

Scrooge's office. Bob Cratchit, a mild-mannered, suffering blob of a man, sits at his desk, shivering and writing in a notebook. Nearby, set off somewhat, is Scrooge's desk. Near his desk two gentlemen in topcoats are standing, waiting for him. Scrooge enters in a bad mood.

BOB CRATCHIT. Good morning, Mr. Scrooge.

EBENEZER SCROOGE. You still alive, Bob Cratchit? You haven't died of pneumonia yet?

BOB CRATCHIT. Well I'm very cold, it's true, Mr. Scrooge. Might we put another coal on the fire?

EBENEZER SCROOGE. No we may not. I am not made of money, Bob Cratchit. A little cold never hurt anyone.

BOB CRATCHIT. I have this sort of pain right in the middle of my chest every time I breathe in the cold air.

EBENEZER SCROOGE. Really? Well when you're about to fall over dead, tell me, so I can go out and hire your replacement.

BOB CRATCHIT. Yes, sir. Oh, Mr. Scrooge, there are two gentlemen to see you, sir.

EBENEZER SCROOGE. What did I tell you about letting people wait for me in my office?

BOB CRATCHIT. You said not to do it.

EBENEZER SCROOGE. And so why did you do it?

BOB CRATCHIT. I have trouble saying no to people, Mr. Scrooge.

EBENEZER SCROOGE. Slap yourself in the face, Bob Cratchit.

BOB CRATCHIT. I'd rather not, Mr. Scrooge.

EBENEZER SCROOGE. Don't say no to me.

BOB CRATCHIT. Very well, sir. *(Bob slaps himself in the face.)*

EBENEZER SCROOGE. Ah, very good. I knew there was some reason I paid you your tiny weekly salary.

BOB CRATCHIT. And why is that, sir?

EBENEZER SCROOGE. You amuse me. Hit yourself again. *(Bob hits himself again.)* Oh very good. You're starting to put me in a good mood. Now, let me go be abusive to the gentlemen in my office. *(Scrooge goes into his office area. The two gentlemen speak to him.)*

GENTLEMAN 1. Good morning, Mr. Scrooge. Merry Christmas.

GENTLEMAN 2. Merry Christmas to you, sir.

EBENEZER SCROOGE. Bah humbug! I want to put bugs in your hair.

GENTLEMAN 1. What kind of bugs, sir?

EBENEZER SCROOGE. Oh, disgusting horrible ones who'll emit some sort of terrible liquid all over your heads. Hahahahaha. And people say I don't have a sense of humor. What is it you want today, bah-humbug, Christmas-stinks-Christmas-carols-make-me-puke.

GENTLEMAN 2. *(Aside to Gentleman 1.)* Goodness, if we lived in another century, I would say this man has Tourette's Syndrome.

GENTLEMAN 1. Mr. Scrooge, we are fellow businessmen collecting for the United Way. And every Christmas we give a little bit from our pockets to all the poor people who wander throughout London in poverty and despair. And we wondered how much we could put you down for?

EBENEZER SCROOGE. Nothing.

GENTLEMAN 1. You wish to be anonymous?

EBENEZER SCROOGE. No, no, no — I wish to give nothing. Let the poor go to workhouses, or orphanages, or die in the street. I am not my brother's keeper. I am a frugal businessman.

GENTLEMAN 1. Might you be interested in selling energy units with us?

EBENEZER SCROOGE. Energy units?

GENTLEMAN 1. Mr. Scrooge, let me introduce myself. I'm Kenneth Lay, and this is my partner Jeffrey Skilling, doesn't he have a scary face? Now let me explain energy units. *(Explains with energy and some speed.)* You see, we take the warmth given off by the candle, say, and we "package" that energy, and then we set up a tax-free corporation in the Bahamas, and then we charge poor people, and the state of California, money for the use of these energy units. And we say there's a shortage and we triple the price, and we mis-state our earnings and expenses, and our scribe Arthur Andersen shreds a lot of documents, and ultimately we make enormous profits without actually offering any services whatsoever. And then we all go bankrupt, and we retire as millionaires!

EBENEZER SCROOGE. Gentlemen, I am extremely impressed. And I think I'd like to join in your business, and sell these "units of energy." Oh, Bob Cratchit, come in here a minute. *(Bob Cratchit comes in.)*

BOB CRATCHIT. Yes, your Grace?

EBENEZER SCROOGE. What is your weekly salary, Bob Cratchit?

BOB CRATCHIT. You pay me eleven shillings, sir.

EBENEZER SCROOGE. Well from now on I am paying you six shillings, Bob.

BOB CRATCHIT. Why is that, sir.

EBENEZER SCROOGE. I'm deducting five shillings from your salary, and purchasing some energy units for you and your family.

BOB CRATCHIT. Thank you, sir. And what are energy units so I may tell hard-working, exhausted Mrs. Cratchit when I see her next?

EBENEZER SCROOGE. Energy units, Bob, are like the warmth from a candle. I know how cold you say you always are, so I'm buying you some heat. And I'm charging you five shillings for it.

BOB CRATCHIT. Energy units and more warmth. Oh I think Mrs. Cratchit will be delighted to hear this, sirs.

EBENEZER SCROOGE. Merry Christmas, Bob, hahaha, humbug, kaplooey.

BOB CRATCHIT. Yes, Mr. Scrooge, thank you very much. *(Bob goes back to his desk.)*

EBENEZER SCROOGE. Our first customer.

GENTLEMAN 1. *(Offers his hand to Scrooge.)* Mr. Scrooge, I believe we've found a business partner.

EBENEZER SCROOGE. Merry Christmas! There, I can say it in celebration as long as it's a nasty thing I'm celebrating. Hooray for more money for me, and less for everybody else!

BOTH GENTLEMEN. Hear, hear, Merry Christmas! *(Lights dim on this scene. The Ghost comes downstage to speak.)*

GHOST. Wasn't that upsetting. And clearly Mr. Scrooge needs to be changed. So what shall we do next? Well, I think a little visit from his ex-business partner Jacob Marley may be in order, don't you? And some scary noises and some rattling chains. Coming right up.

Scene 3

Scrooge's house. A big wingback chair. Not much else. Maybe a clock on a wall. Enter Scrooge.

EBENEZER SCROOGE. Energy units, what a joke. Oh how I enjoy how stupid people are. Bob Cratchit, you and your children will freeze as much as always and I've cut your salary in half, and you'll thank me for it. Hahahaha. Bah humbug. Now let me sit in my favorite chair and read the announcements of the next public executions. *(He sits in his chair, looks at a printed list.)* Ah, next Tuesday, right after breakfast. I can make that one. Ah, my previous housekeeper, put to death for stealing. I will certainly make that one. *(Offstage, the sound of some ghostly "woooo-ing.")*

OFFSTAGE GHOSTS. Woooooooo-ooooo.

EBENEZER SCROOGE. What is that, I wonder?

OFFSTAGE GHOSTS. Wooooooooo-oooooo!

EBENEZER SCROOGE. It must be my imagination. *(Enter two ghosts, both dressed pathetically, with a "ghostly" sheet with a hole for their heads to poke through; and with a white piece of cloth wrapped from their chin to the top of their heads. Perhaps they both have socks with garters. One ghost is the size of a man; the other is small, the size of a child. They are Jacob Marley's Ghost and Young Jacob Marley from earlier, now dressed as a ghost.)*

THE MARLEY GHOSTS. Wooooooo-oooooo. Wooooooooooo-ooooooo.

EBENEZER SCROOGE. Oh Lord, what is this?

JACOB MARLEY'S GHOST. Do you recognize me, Ebenezer?

EBENEZER SCROOGE. Not really.

JACOB MARLEY'S GHOST. Ebenezer, I am your business partner Jacob Marley, dead these many years.

EBENEZER SCROOGE. Well who dressed you, you look ridiculous.

JACOB MARLEY'S GHOST. I am condemned to wander the earth, day after day, mourning my past mistakes, never to find rest or peace. *(Emits a surprisingly loud cry of anguish.)* OOOOO-OOOOOOOOOOOOOOOOOOOOOOOOOHHHHHHHHHHH!

YOUNG JACOB. There, there, older self. Don't feel bad.

EBENEZER SCROOGE. Is this young boy your servant?

JACOB MARLEY'S GHOST. He is my tormentor!

EBENEZER SCROOGE. He teases you?

JACOB MARLEY'S GHOST. He torments me because I see how sweetly I began, and how empty and callous I ended.

EBENEZER SCROOGE. Yes, yes, I see. I'm getting bored with your visit, can you leave?

JACOB MARLEY'S GHOST. You are not afraid to speak to a ghost that way?

EBENEZER SCROOGE. Well, are you a ghost? I think you could as easily be a piece of undigested mutton. Or some stomach-churning, unfinished glob of fermenting Rice-A-Roni.

YOUNG JACOB. The San Francisco treat.

EBENEZER SCROOGE. He has few lines, but enjoys the ones he has. Very good, young man, well spoken.

JACOB MARLEY'S GHOST. *(Emphatic, full of ghostly scariness.)* Scrooooooooooge! I come with a warning. Unless you mend your ways, you will be condemned to the same fate as me — to walk the earth in torment for all your days. Wooooooooooooooo-ooooo, woe —

EBENEZER SCROOGE. *(Glib, wanting to be rid of him.)* All right, fine, I'll change. Okay?

JACOB MARLEY'S GHOST. Ebenezer, you will be visited three times tonight by three separate spirits — or possibly just one spirit, who will come three separate times and change its name each time. Either way, those spirits are your one and only chance to save yourself and escape your horrible fate.

EBENEZER SCROOGE. Fine, fine, you've made point. Please let me rest now.

JACOB MARLEY'S GHOST. The first spirit will come when the clock strikes one. The second spirit will come when the clock strikes two. The third spir ...

EBENEZER SCROOGE. *(Starts pushing them out.)* Yes, yes, I get where you're going, thank you for coming. Goodbye, Jacob Marley. Goodbye, mini-Marley. Goodbye, goodbye, goodbye. *(Scrooge gets the Marley ghosts offstage. But immediately Jacob Marley's Ghost comes back.)*

JACOB MARLEY'S GHOST. *(Emphatic, needing to complete his thought.)* The third spirit will come when the clock strikes three !!! *(Glares, exits. Scrooge sits back in his chair, suddenly exhausted.)*

EBENEZER SCROOGE. Oh, I am suddenly exhausted! How odd. *(His body shifts abruptly, he suddenly nods off to a total sleep.)*

Scene 4

Lights change. A clock strikes one. Scrooge opens his eyes.

EBENEZER SCROOGE. Oh. The clock strikes one. Oh dear. I don't want to see a ghost. *(Enter the Ghost. She is dressed as a UPS delivery man.)*

GHOST. UPS delivery. UPS delivery. Oh, Mr. Scrooge, I have a package.

EBENEZER SCROOGE. Really? I was expecting a ghost. But a UPS delivery person is a welcome relief. What is it?

GHOST. A Christmas present from all your grateful friends and relatives. *(She offers him a package … but wrapped like a festive Christmas gift, not like a UPS package.)*

EBENEZER SCROOGE. Really? That doesn't seem very likely. *(Opens it.)* Ah. A pair of socks. How fascinating. Bah humbug!

GHOST. Mr. Scrooge, I am the Ghost of Christmas Past.

EBENEZER SCROOGE. And you're reduced to delivering packages?

GHOST. Yes, but with a purpose. Because I am here to teach you various lessons so you can improve your manner of keeping Christmas.

EBENEZER SCROOGE. Oh, you keep Christmas, leave me out of it.

GHOST. First of all, the way you receive presents is just no good. Try it again. *(Offers him a second identical package.)* Now before opening, you must proclaim in loud and grateful tones how lovely the wrapping is.

EBENEZER SCROOGE. I don't want to. *(The Ghost reaches over with an electrical zapper and zaps him.)*

ELECTRICAL ZAPPER. Zap! Zap!

EBENEZER SCROOGE. Aaaaaaaagggggghh! What is that?

GHOST. That is an energy unit that we in the afterlife have fashioned into a zapper. And it zaps painful jolting electric currents through your body. And if you disobey, I shall use it again and again and again.

EBENEZER SCROOGE. O Lord.

GHOST. Now as I said, I want you to make a big fuss over the Christmas wrapping. *(Scrooge stares at her with annoyance. She brandishes the zapper again. He gives in, decides to do what she says.)*
EBENEZER SCROOGE. *(With feigned, if slightly unconvincing, delight.)* Oh … what a lovely package. It is so, so very nice. Very, very, very, very nice.
GHOST. Be more specific.
EBENEZER SCROOGE. It's so … colorful. I love the ribbon on it. Ummm … what a lovely shade of yellow it is. Makes me think of egg yolk, makes me think of vomit. *(She zaps him.)* Aaaaaaaaggghhhh! Makes me think of daffodils. Lovely, lovely daffodils. What a wonderful package. I … I … hate even to open it, it's so lovely.
GHOST. Much better. Now open it, and then gush about the gift.
EBENEZER SCROOGE. All right. *(While he starts to open it.)* What do you think is in it? It's too light to be a book. It's too small to be a … cast-iron statue of Oliver Cromwell. What do you think it is? Shall I see? *(Opens it; takes out a pair of white gym socks.)* Oh, how marvellous! Socks! Just what I need. I love socks. Thank you so very, very, very much.
GHOST. That was so-so. Gush some more.
EBENEZER SCROOGE. Ummmm. I love white socks. They're so … clean. And useful. I'm thrilled out of my mind. Out of my mind, I tell you. Is that enough? Can I stop talking about the socks please???
GHOST. Yes, you may. For I am the Ghost of Christmas Past, and we have visiting to do. First off, I think we shall go to the Fezziwigs.
EBENEZER SCROOGE. Oh not those loud, awful bores.
GHOST. The very ones. Come touch my arm and the set shall change around us.
EBENEZER SCROOGE. Very well. *(Scrooge touches the Ghost's arm, and there are air rustling sounds, like racing through space and time. And the set changes around them and we find ourselves at:)*

Scene 5

Bob Cratchit's house. A wooden table, missing a leg but standing nonetheless; it seats perhaps six. A chair or two. Mrs. Bob Cratchit is there, doing needlepoint. A couple of children lie on the floor (a girl and boy). Scrooge and the Ghost stand in the set, staring at them.

CHILD 1. *(Girl.)* I'm hungry.

CHILD 2. *(Boy.)* Me too.

MRS. BOB CRATCHIT. So we're all hungry. What do you want me to do about it?

CHILD 1. Give us some food.

EBENEZER SCROOGE. This isn't the Fezziwigs.

GHOST. You're right, it's not. I seem to have brought us to the wrong place.

MRS. BOB CRATCHIT. Excuse me, who are you?

GHOST. Uh … no one. I'm a ghost. You can't see me.

EBENEZER SCROOGE. And I'm just some old man. *(Whispers to Ghost.)* Why can she see us?

GHOST. I don't know, something's wrong. *(To Mrs. Bob Cratchit.)* We were looking for the Fezziwigs.

MRS. BOB CRATCHIT. Oh? And who might they be?

GHOST. They were employers of Mr. Scroo … of this old gentleman long ago. Tell me, is this the present or the past?

MRS. BOB CRATCHIT. Every day of my life seems the same to me, I haven't a clue if it's the present or the past. Children, are we in the present or the past?

CHILD 1. I'm hungry.

CHILD 2. Feed us!

MRS. BOB CRATCHIT. All children want to do is eat, it's disgusting. *(Screams at them.)* When your father finally makes some money, then you'll eat! And not a minute before!

GHOST. Oh right, this is Bob Cratchit's house, isn't it?

MRS. BOB CRATCHIT. What?

GHOST. We're supposed to be here much later. Something's gone awry.

MRS. BOB CRATCHIT. I'm sorry, who are you and why are you here?

GHOST. *(To Scrooge.)* Touch my cloak and I'll try to get us back in time to the Fezziwigs.

EBENEZER SCROOGE. What cloak?

GHOST. My arm then, don't be so fussy. Touch my arm. *(Scrooge touches the Ghost's arm and there's a large POP sound. Brief flash of light too. But Scrooge and the Ghost are still there.)*

MRS. BOB CRATCHIT. Oh! Where did those two go? The black delivery woman and the old doddering man. Children, did you see them leave?

CHILD 1. I'm hungry.

MRS. BOB CRATCHIT. Shut up. That's strange, I didn't see them leave.

GHOST. Well at least we're invisible now. That part is working again. Touch my arm again, and I'll try to get us to the Fezziwigs. *(Scrooge touches her arm. Nothing.)* Damn it, I don't know what's the matter.

MRS. BOB CRATCHIT. Children, don't swear.

GHOST. We're here at the Cratchit house way too early.

CHILD 2. Father and Tiny Tim are home, I think.

MRS. BOB CRATCHIT. I wonder what good news your father will have for Christmas Eve. Maybe Scrooge will have died and named us in his will, ha ha ha.

EBENEZER SCROOGE. That's rather rude.

MRS. BOB CRATCHIT. *(To the children.)* Did you say something?

CHILD 1. No. We didn't say anything.

MRS. BOB CRATCHIT. I thought I heard a voice. Oh Lord, I'm hearing things now.

EBENEZER SCROOGE. Can they hear us?

GHOST. They're not supposed to. *(Enter Bob Cratchit and Tiny Tim. Bob has a long, long scarf around his neck that falls to the ground. Tiny Tim is small, carries a little crutch, and limps a lot.)*

BOB CRATCHIT. Gladys, darling, we're home. And Tiny Tim so enjoyed looking in the store windows at all the Christmas treats he can't have.

TINY TIM. And I only fell on the ground twenty-four times today.

MRS. BOB CRATCHIT. Why won't you use your crutch, you stupid child?

TINY TIM. I don't want to people to notice I'm crippled.

MRS. BOB CRATCHIT. And if you fall down twenty-four times,

you don't think they'll notice?

TINY TIM. Leave me alone.

BOB CRATCHIT. Let poor Tiny Tim alone, dear. He's a sensitive soul.

MRS. BOB CRATCHIT. That damn crutch cost half of your weekly salary, and the idiot child won't use it.

TINY TIM. I don't need it!

GHOST. Isn't this a sad family? Do you feel sorry for them?

MRS. BOB CRATCHIT. Did you hear that?

BOB CRATCHIT. Hear what, my darling?

MRS. BOB CRATCHIT. I heard some voice saying we're a sad family.

BOB CRATCHIT. Oh, and so we are, and proud of it. I see the people on the street point at me and Tiny Tim, and they say, "Look, there goes that man who hasn't money to feed his twenty children, and there's his little cripple child. But he's a kind man," they say.

MRS. BOB CRATCHIT. If we have so little money, why do you keep adopting children?

BOB CRATCHIT. I love children. Where are the children?

MRS. BOB CRATCHIT. They're all in a bunch in the root cellar. *(Bob opens a trap door and calls down to presumably a horde of children.)*

BOB CRATCHIT. Merry Christmas, children! I hope you're all well and happy!

MANY VOICES. *(Perhaps recorded on tape; in unison.)* We're hungry!

CHILD 1 and CHILD 2. We're hungry too!

BOB CRATCHIT. Children are always so hungry, it's kind of cute. Oh, my Lord, I forgot … *(Bob runs to the main door, and goes out it.)*

TINY TIM. Father has a Christmas surprise for you, mother. *(Bob comes running back in with a bundle, wrapped in a blanket.)*

BOB CRATCHIT. Look, darling, another foundling. I found a foundling.

MRS. BOB CRATCHIT. And what do you want me to do with it? Cook it for Christmas dinner in place of the goose we don't have?

CHILD 1 and CHILD 2. We're hungry. Feed us!

MRS. BOB CRATCHIT. We're not cannibals yet, children. Soon, but not yet.

EBENEZER SCROOGE. Oh what a gruesome family.

MRS. BOB CRATCHIT. Did you hear that?

BOB CRATCHIT. Hear what?

MRS. BOB CRATCHIT. Someone said we were gruesome.

BOB CRATCHIT. I didn't hear anything.

MRS. BOB CRATCHIT. Maybe I'm losing my mind. That would be a nice Christmas present.

GHOST. We really should be at the Fezziwigs.

MRS. BOB CRATCHIT. Bob Cratchit, we already have twenty other children, all of whom have to sleep in a great big pile in the root cellar and rarely have enough to eat. Are you out of your mind, bringing another child into this house? *(Bob hands the bundle to Mrs. Bob.)*

BOB CRATCHIT. But you so love children, my darling.

MRS. BOB CRATCHIT. Love children? Are you stupid as well as poor? *(To the two children on the ground.)* Children, do I act like I like children?

CHILD 1 and CHILD 2. No, mother.

TINY TIM. Indeed she does not. Mother often tears at her hair and cries out, "Oh what a wretched life I lead with twenty children."

MRS. BOB CRATCHIT. And now twenty-one! *(Stands and screams.)* God, strike me dead now, I don't want to live.

EBENEZER SCROOGE. Goodness. Why are you showing me this?

GHOST. I have no idea.

MRS. BOB CRATCHIT. Bob Cratchit, did you ask that horrible Mr. Scrooge for a raise as I told you to?

BOB CRATCHIT. Well an amusing story about that ... I was going to, when Mr. Scrooge called me in and told me that he was buying us all energy units of heat out of half of my existing salary.

MRS. BOB CRATCHIT. What? Energy units of heat? And he's using HALF of your salary to buy whatever these things are? I may go mad right now. I'll go nuts, I'll go crackers.

CHILD 1. I want a cracker.

CHILD 2. I want a cracker.

BOB CRATCHIT. Listen to the children, they're so cute.

GHOST. Poor Mrs. Cratchit. She's losing her mind due to your business practices.

EBENEZER SCROOGE. Oh pooey. If she ends up in Bedlam, that's her problem.

MRS. BOB CRATCHIT. I'm hearing voices talk about me. They say I'm ready for Bedlam. And I am too.

BOB CRATCHIT. Oh there's not a saner woman in all of London.

MRS. BOB CRATCHIT. You're missing part of your brain, aren't you? Open the root cellar door, would you? *(Bob opens the trap door again. Mrs. Bob goes over to it. Calling down to the children.)* Children, here's a new little brother or sister for you. Give it a name and take care of it, would you? *(Mrs. Bob Cratchit starts to toss the foundling down there, but Bob stops her.)*

BOB CRATCHIT. Gladys, darling, what are you doing? This is an infant. You mustn't throw it down to the cellar. We must cherish it.

MRS. BOB CRATCHIT. Oh, right, cherish it. *(To the foundling.)* Hello, little child. Cherish, cherish, cherish. *(Hands Bob the child.)* Here, you cherish the child a while, would you? I think I want to go get a drink at the pub and then jump off London Bridge. *(Calls down to the root cellar.)* Goodbye, children. Mother's going to jump off the bridge. Do as I say and not as I do. Have a nice Christmas dinner tomorrow.

TINY TIM. Oh, Mummy, don't die!

MRS. BOB CRATCHIT. Don't tell me what to do!

CHILD 1 and CHILD 2. Mummy! Mummy!

MRS. BOB CRATCHIT. Goodbye, everyone! I can't stand being alive one more second! *(Mrs. Bob Cratchit rushes out of the house.)*

BOB CRATCHIT. Gladys, please don't do this. It's Christmas Eve! It's a happy time.

TINY TIM. Where's Mummy going? How can she leave me, her little crippled child? Not to mention the new foundling, the two children sitting over there, and the remaining children in the root cellar?

BOB CRATCHIT. Oh what a long question that was, Tiny Tim, and I have not an answer for you. Oh it breaks my heart. I think we all better cry for your unhappy lot. On the count of three, everybody weep. One, two, three. *(Bob, Tiny Tim, and the two children all weep.)*

EBENEZER SCROOGE. *(Uncomfortable.)* Oh, Lord, they're crying. *(Lights dim on the Cratchits. The Ghost and Scrooge walk to another part of the stage.)* That was very pathetic. If I weren't so heartless, I would've been moved. But I wasn't. And why *does* he keep bringing children home when they have no money? And don't you agree, Mrs. Cratchit seems in serious trouble?

GHOST. I don't mean to be rigid, but we're supposed to go to the Fezziwigs *first,* so you can be reminded of your cheerful, Dickensian boss who was so generous and full of life and showed us all the joyful side of Christmas. We're not supposed to have witnessed any of what we just saw, and I can't let it distract us.

EBENEZER SCROOGE. I think I should go back to bed, and

you should go back to Ghost School or something. *(Scrooge starts to walk away.)*

GHOST. Ebenezer Scrooge, you come back here. We have got to make you change your personality by the end of this evening. Now admittedly we've had trouble getting things off to a proper start, but you're not to go back to bed. Though perhaps going back to your residence might be right ... maybe I can get my astral directions working again, and then we can move on to the Fezziwigs. They're usually quite an audience favorite, and there's no point in depressing everyone with that sour rendition of Mrs. Bob Cratchit which is nowhere to be found in Dickens.

EBENEZER SCROOGE. Oh very well. Let's walk back to my place, shall we? What an idiotic ghost. *(The Ghost zaps Scrooge as they both exit.)*

Scene 6

A pub. Various people milling around. A bartender. Everyone is singing a carol.

EVERYONE.
GOOD KING WENCESLAUS LOOKED OUT,
ON THE FEAST OF STEPHEN,
AS THE SNOW LAY DEEP ABOUT,
DUH DUH DUH AND EVEN,
DUH DUH THE MOON THAT NIGHT
WHEN THE WIND WAS CRU-EL
DUH DUH DUH DUH CAME IN SIGHT
SERVING CHRISTMAS GRU-UEL ...

(They kind of know they don't know it. Mrs. Bob Cratchit sort of explodes into the room.)

MRS. BOB CRATCHIT. I NEED A DRINK! *(The bartender gives her a shot of something, which she drinks quickly.)* Hit me again! *(She gulps the second shot down.)* And again! *(Gulps the third shot down.)* Okay. I'll let it kick in, and then I'll want directions to London Bridge. *(The Ghost and Scrooge suddenly arrive.)*

GHOST. At last! And now — the Fezziwigs! *(The Ghost and*

25

Scrooge look around. No Fezziwigs in sight.) Gosh darn it! Come on, get a move on here, I demand to conjure up the FEZZIWIGS! *(Great noise and commotion. Lights go out, and flash around. Everyone in the pub sort of scurries on and offstage; clearly something is happening. Maybe the sounds of alarm bells ringing too. When the lights settle back on, the set is more or less the same, except a Christmas tree has been brought on … the people in the pub have put on different accents to their costumes — festive hats? or Christmas tinsel around their necks, or something. And significantly — Mr. and Mrs. Fezziwig are there. They are dressed [and padded] to look like a male and female Tweedledee and Tweedledum; they have bright orange wigs on and look extremely "Dickensian" in a clichéd, over-the-top way. They are extremely cheerful and happy, they dominate the room.)*

MR. and MRS. FEZZIWIG. MERRY CHRISTMAS, ONE AND ALL, FROM YOUR FRIENDS AND EMPLOYERS, THE FEZZIWIGS!

MRS. FEZZIWIG. And God bless us, every one!

MRS. BOB CRATCHIT. Tiny Tim says that!

MRS. FEZZIWIG. Tiny who? *(Mrs. Cratchit looks around confused. She's not sure where she is. She knows it's not quite the pub she walked into a minute ago, but she also knows she's a bit drunk, and doesn't know where she is.)*

MRS. BOB CRATCHIT. Where am I, I wonder? Things looks different.

MR. FEZZIWIG. It's time to stop work, everyone. You too, Ebenezer Scrooge, you too, Dick Wilkins. Everyone get ready to drink some Christmas punch, spiked with a little Christmas cheer, and get ready to dance a merry ol' dance with our two matrimonially available daughters. *(The two matrimonially available Fezziwig daughters enter just now, and grin at everyone, very happy and very available.)*

EBENEZER SCROOGE. Yes, it's good ol' Mr. Fezziwig. I recognize him indeed. I and Dick Wilkins were apprentices to him when we were young men.

GHOST. Thank goodness, we finally got here! It's the past. And I am the Ghost of Christmas Past, and that's where we are. Phew!!!

MRS. BOB CRATCHIT. Where's the Christmas punch? Give me some punch!

EBENEZER SCROOGE. Oh, Lord. Why is she here?

GHOST. I don't know. She shouldn't be here. It's some glitch or other. Just pay her no attention.

MRS. BOB CRATCHIT. Some glitch? Oh I'm hearing voices again. *(Hits her head with her hand.)* Shut up, shut up!

GHOST. The lesson for you to learn is about how well the Fezziwigs celebrate Christmas, and how they make it fun for their employees. Can you focus on that please?

EBENEZER SCROOGE. Well, I'll try.

MRS. BOB CRATCHIT. I need some punch please!

MR. FEZZIWIG. Get this woman some punch! *(Someone hands Mrs. Bob Cratchit a glass of punch. She gulps it.)*

MRS. BOB CRATCHIT. Mmmmm, delicious. Good. Now as soon as I'm really drunk, I want to kill myself.

MR. FEZZIWIG. Ha ha ha, that's a dark bit of humor there, now now, killing oneself is for other days, not for Christmas, and not for Christmas Eve. Am I right, Mrs. Fezziwig?

MRS. FEZZIWIG. You're right, Mr. Fezziwig. Holidays are wonderful things. And Christmas is the most wonderful holiday of them all. And why is that, Mr. Fezziwig?

MR. FEZZIWIG. Well, I'll tell you, Mrs. Fezziwig. *(The Fezziwigs are just so darn happy they can't help but sing a song. It eventually builds to everyone joining in joyfully, even Scrooge, who has fond memories of his apprenticeship. The only one who doesn't join in is Mrs. Bob Cratchit, who stays over by the punch bowl. Or gets pushed around the stage haphazardly when dance movements take over.)*

  BE HAPPY AND PERKY
  YOU'RE GONNA EAT TURKEY
  BE SNIPPY AND SNAPPY
  'CAUSE CHRISTMAS IS HAPPY

  SCREAM OUT, BE ELATED
  EAT UP 'TIL YOU'RE SATED
  BE ZESTFUL AND ZINGY AND TANGY AND GAY

MR. and MRS. FEZZIWIG.
  EAT, DRINK AND BE MERRY
  PLAY GAMES UNDER MISTLETOE BERRY
  EAT, DRINK AND BE JOLLY
  RUN MAD, HANG SOME TINSEL AND HOLLY
  IT'S CHRISTMAS AND WE'RE GLAD
  THE OPPOSITE OF SAD
  WITH JOY WE MAY GO MAD

MR. FEZZIWIG.
    SEE NOW, SNOW IS FALLING,
    THE FIDDLER IS CALLING
    OUTSIDE, TREES ARE FROSTED
    GOOD GOD, I'M EXHAUSTED!
(Holds heart a bit, short of breath.)
MRS. FEZZIWIG and EVERYONE.
    CHRISTMAS, CHRISTMAS, CHRISTMAS!
(Mrs. Fezziwig helps Mr. Fezziwig stand up straight again, and he sings the next part with renewed vigor.)

MR. FEZZIWIG.
    BE LIVELY AND FRISKY
    YOU'RE GONNA DRINK WHISKEY
MRS. FEZZIWIG.
    GO MARCHING AND DRUMMING
    'CAUSE CHRISTMAS IS COMING
MR. FEZZIWIG.
    GET PLASTERED AND TIPSY
    AND DANCE LIKE A GYPSY
MRS. FEZZIWIG.
    BE ZESTFUL AND ZINGY AND TANGY AND TINGY
        AND PUCKISH
    AND PINGY AND GAY

MR. and MRS. FEZZIWIG and EVERYONE.
    EAT, DRINK AND BE MERRY
    PLAY GAMES UNDER MISTLETOE BERRY
    EAT, DRINK AND BE JOLLY
    RUN MAD, HANG SOME TINSEL AND HOLLY

    IT'S CHRISTMAS AND WE'RE GLAD
    THE OPPOSITE OF SAD
    WITH JOY WE MAY GO MAD
    'CAUSE WE'RE FILLED WITH GLEE AND JOY AND
        CHEER

    CHRISTMAS, CHRISTMAS, CHRISTMAS, CHRISTMAS,
    CHRISTMAS, CHRISTMAS, CHRISTMAS!
(The Fezziwigs and everyone else are so happy and overheated that they have to lie down on the floor, panting happily.)

MR. FEZZIWIG. Oh my God, I'm having a heart attack. *(Mrs. Fezziwig gives her husband mouth-to-mouth resuscitation, then pounds on his chest.)*

GHOST. Oh my God. *(To Scrooge.)* Did he die in the past?

EBENEZER SCROOGE. I don't think so. I would've remembered, wouldn't I? I hope I would've.

MRS. FEZZIWIG. It's all right, everyone, Mr. Fezziwig is coming back to life again.

MR. FEZZIWIG. *(Sitting up.)* Oh, my goodness, that was a close one. Bring me some punch and pastry.

MRS. FEZZIWIG. Yes, he needs his strength. Bring him alcohol and pastries right away. Oh every Christmas he nearly dies of a heart attack, but he just can't help but show people how to have a good time at Christmas.

GHOST. Good, well that's the point I was hoping to make.

MRS. BOB CRATCHIT. Okay, I'm ready to die now. Which way to London Bridge?

GHOST. Now, Mrs. Cratchit, can you hear me?

MRS. BOB CRATCHIT. Yes, you're in my head all right.

GHOST. Now listen to me. You need Paxil or Zoloft. Are you on an antidepressant?

MRS. BOB CRATCHIT. On a what?

GHOST. Oh that's right, I'm ahead of myself again. Well, just go home to Mr. Cratchit. I'm trying to redeem this man here and you're part of his story. If you kill yourself, the story has an entirely different meaning.

MRS. BOB CRATCHIT. Story? I don't know what you're talking about. Which way to the river?

EBENEZER SCROOGE. Oh, let her kill herself, and I'll just go home to bed.

GHOST. No! You will not go back to bed. You are on a journey and we're going to get it right. Now I've showed you your childhood, and I've showed the Fezziwigs …

EBENEZER SCROOGE. You haven't shown me my childhood.

GHOST. Yes, I have. Oh my God, I haven't? *(Mrs. Bob Cratchit starts to creep out.)*

MRS. BOB CRATCHIT. I'll find the river myself. Good night everyone. Merry Christmas, see you in hell! *(Exits.)*

MRS. FEZZIWIG. Did she say "see you in hell"? That's a terrible Christmas greeting.

GHOST. Oh God, we've got to go back and do his childhood …

Scrooge, hold my arm … we're going back, back, back … *(Everyone onstage makes a woo-woo sound, the lights go strange and we're back in time.)*

Scene 7

Young Ebenezer and Young Jacob stand next to one another, as in the first scene. The Ghost and Scrooge watch them. No one else is onstage.

YOUNG JACOB.
  HARK THE HERALD ANGELS SING,
  GLORY TO THE NEWBORN KING,
YOUNG EBENEZER. Bah! Humbug!
GHOST. Young Ebenezer hated Christmas from an early age.
YOUNG EBENEZER. It's too commercial! And it's icky and goody-goody. I hate it!
GHOST. Poor Ebenezer grew up in an orphanage.
EBENEZER SCROOGE. No, I didn't.
GHOST. Yes, you did. *(A man and a woman, the Beadle and his Wife, enter with a big pot and a big ladle. The Beadle holds the pot; his Wife holds the ladle. The Beadle and his Wife are played by the same actors who played Mr. and Mrs. Fezziwig, but they've taken off their red wigs and done a few other minor costume adjustments.)*
BEADLE. Come get your porridge, you ungrateful orphan children.
WIFE. So-weeeee! So-weeeeeee! Come along, little piggies! *(The Wife ladles porridge into bowls, which Young Ebenezer and Young Jacob hold out to her. Ladling it out:)* Here's glop for you, and glop for you. Now, choke on it! *(Young Ebenezer and Young Jacob mime gobbling up their oatmeal.)*
GHOST. Isn't it sad? The poor, poor children in this horrible orphanage.
BEADLE. The children should be very grateful for the food we give them, isn't that so, Mrs. Fezziwig?
WIFE. My name isn't Mrs. Fezziwig.
BEADLE. No, of course, it's not. It's something else. Mrs. Cratchit?
WIFE. No, I can't remember what my name is, but it isn't Mrs.

30

Cratchit. Oh look, one of the young boys is coming over to us. *(Young Ebenezer walks over to the Beadle and holds out his empty bowl.)*
YOUNG EBENEZER. Please, sir … I want some more.
BEADLE. What???
YOUNG EBENEZER. Please, sir … I want some … more?
EBENEZER SCROOGE. None of this rings a bell.
GHOST. Well it's your childhood.
EBENEZER SCROOGE. I don't remember it.
GHOST. Well, you've repressed it.
WIFE. He wants more!! Oliver Twist, you are an ungrateful child!
EBENEZER SCROOGE. You see, she said another name. You've taken me to some other person's past, you incompetent fool.
GHOST. She didn't say Oliver Twist. She said Ebenezer Scrooge.
EBENEZER SCROOGE. I heard her say Oliver Twist.
WIFE. Ebenezer Scrooge, you are an ungrateful child. I don't know why I said Oliver Twist. Maybe the other child is Oliver Twist.
YOUNG JACOB. No. I'm Jacob Marley.
WIFE. Jacob Marley … I don't remember having an orphan by that name here.
BEADLE. I think you're Mrs. Fezziwig.
WIFE. Well I'm not. You're the Beadle and I'm Mrs. Beadle.
BEADLE. If you say so.
EBENEZER SCROOGE. *(To Ghost.)* I think you don't know what you're doing.
GHOST. Look, the point is, you were either an orphan or you weren't, but you had a tough life, it helped to make you the mean, mean man you became. Okay? Point made … let's not get hung up on whether all the details are exactly right or not. All right?
EBENEZER SCROOGE. I think you're incompetent.
GHOST. Well I think you're mean and stingy and a terrible person. *(Zaps him with the zapper.)*
EBENEZER SCROOGE. Aaaaaaaaagggghhhh!
GHOST. And now that's the end of my tenure as the Ghost of Christmas Past. You go back to sleep for a while, and the Ghost of Christmas Present will show up shortly.
BEADLE. And where do we go?
GHOST. You go to the kitchen, to wash out that disgusting pot.
BEADLE. All right.
WIFE. Let's make the children wash the pot! And scrub the floor too!
YOUNG EBENEZER. I don't want to scrub the floor!
WIFE. Oliver Twist, you're a lazy bum. You'll be fired from your

first job.

YOUNG EBENEZER. Not if I'm self-employed I won't be.

WIFE. Shut up! *(The Beadle and his Wife exit, followed by Young Ebenezer and Young Jacob.)*

GHOST. Minions of the night, send Mr. Scrooge back to sleep. *(Ghost exits. Lights, music. A couple of "minions of the night" — or townsfolk — help with the set change and move Scrooge back to his "home." Scrooge's chair comes back. The minions push Scrooge to it, and he sits in it. If you like, the minions can be stagehands, dressed in their normal clothes.)*

MINIONS OF THE NIGHT. One o'clock, one o'clock, one forty-five. Scrooge is sleepy, Scrooge is sleepy. *(Note: "One o'clock, one o'clock" is in rhythm of "patty-cake, patty-cake.")*

EBENEZER SCROOGE. Why yes, I believe I am. *(Falls asleep abruptly.)*

MINIONS OF THE NIGHT. Sleep in your chair. We don't have a set for the bed. Fall back asleep. *(The minions exit.)*

Scene 8

Scrooge back in his chair. He nods asleep. The clock strikes two. He awakens abruptly.

EBENEZER SCROOGE. Two dings from the clock. That means two A.M. and a second spirit. But here I am in my chair, and all is well. I'm just having bad dreams, clearly. All that stuff about Jacob Marley and the Ghost of Christmas Past. It's just a dream. *(Enter the Ghost again. Lights, magic music. She is now out of her UPS costume. She is in some big robe, with a garland of Christmasy greens on her head. She also has a pretty fake-looking beard on. She's now the Ghost of Christmas Present; and in movies that figure is often presented as a jolly, bearded man with a fancy robe.)*

GHOST. Ho, ho, ho! Ha, ha, ha! I am the Ghost of Christmas Present!

EBENEZER SCROOGE. Oh God. I've had enough of this.

GHOST. Ebenezer Scrooge, you are being given this opportunity to improve yourself.

EBENEZER SCROOGE. All right, all right. Why do you have a beard now?

GHOST. I don't know, I'm Father Christmas. *(Takes off the beard, a bit annoyed with it.)* Here, touch my cloak, we are to look at the ways in which touching, small people celebrate Christmas all over the world.

EBENEZER SCROOGE. Little lessons. I'm not a four-year old.

GHOST. Mr. Scrooge, look at this lovely Dutch couple. *(Enter Mr. and Mrs. Dutch couple. Mrs. Dutch is bald. They have strong Dutch accents.)*

MR. DUTCH PERSON. Merry Christmas, Mrs. Johanson.

MRS. DUTCH PERSON. Merry Christmas, my darling husband. Even though we have no money, I have managed to buy you a Christmas gift, darling Edvar. Look — a watch fob for the cherished timepiece that your father gave you.

MR. DUTCH PERSON. *(Bit disappointed.)* Oh thank you.

MRS. DUTCH PERSON. You don't like it?

MR. DUTCH PERSON. I like it very much, it's just … well, I'm afraid I sold my watch to pay for my present for you.

GHOST. *(To Scrooge.)* I hope you're taking this in?

EBENEZER SCROOGE. Why is she bald?

GHOST. I don't know, be quiet.

MRS. DUTCH PERSON. Oh, Edvar, you bought me a Christmas gift by selling your watch. I am so touched. What did you get me?

MR. DUTCH PERSON. I got you a beautiful comb to wear in your lovely hair. *(He hands her the comb; looks at her.)* Oh my God! Where is your hair?

MRS. DUTCH PERSON. Oh, Edvar. I sold my hair in order to buy you a Christmas present.

MR. DUTCH PERSON. You sold your hair that you love and value more than life itself?

MRS. DUTCH PERSON. Yes, I did.

MR. DUTCH PERSON. Oh, Hedwig! This is so tragic!

MRS. DUTCH PERSON. Oh, Edvar! It is. We've both given up things we love in order to buy presents which are now useless. How I hate Christmas.

MR. DUTCH PERSON. I hate Christmas too, Hedvig. Come, let us go into the other room and kill ourselves.

MRS. DUTCH PERSON. I'd love to. But I sold my father's gun last year to buy you arrows, don't you remember?

MR. DUTCH PERSON. Oh right. Except I could not use the

arrows because I had sold the bow to buy a copper bracelet for your arthritis.

MRS. DUTCH PERSON. And, of course, I don't have arthritis. Darling, wait! We still have the arrows! Why don't we impale ourselves on them as a way of dying?

MR. DUTCH PERSON. Marvelous idea!

GHOST. Stop, stop, stop. This is all wrong! Go away, go away. *(The Ghost pushes the two people off.)* That's not the proper story. I knew something was wrong when their names were Edvar and Hedvig. That story isn't about suicidal Dutch people.

EBENEZER SCROOGE. It was a good story though. And I agree with the meaning — Christmas is stupid and makes us do stupid, awful things.

GHOST. Oh Lord ... no, that's wrong. *(Zaps him with zapper.)*

EBENEZER SCROOGE. Aaaaaaaaagggghhhhh!

GHOST. Now forget everything they said, would you? Oh God. This isn't going like it's supposed to. Okay, we've done Fezziwig, we went back and sort of did your childhood, we've seen Christmas celebrated round the world. NOW is when we're supposed to go to Bob Cratchit's house.

EBENEZER SCROOGE. Oh not the Cratchits again. I'm going to fire that man first thing in the morning, I never want to see him again.

GHOST. You may not live through the morning. Now touch my cloak.

EBENEZER SCROOGE. The Cratchits. What a bunch of crap.

GHOST. Shut up.

Scene 9

The Cratchit house arrives back. Still the table with three legs. There is a pathetic Christmas tree — tiny, few limbs, with like three Christmas balls hung on it and a few strands of tinsel on one branch.

Bob is singing a carol with the children — Tiny Tim, and Child 1 and Child 2. It's "Silent Night." They are singing it at a normal, slightly slow tempo.

BOB and CHILDREN.
   SILENT NIGHT, HOLY NIGHT,
ALL IS CALM …
BOB. Sing it slower, children. Drag it out.
BOB and CHILDREN. *(They all sing really slowly.)*
   ALL IS BRIGHT.
   ROUND YON VIRGIN, MOTHER AND CHILD …
EBENEZER SCROOGE. *(During the singing above.)* Oh God, make them stop that.
GHOST. It's a beloved Christmas song.
BOB and CHILDREN. *(Singing, dirge-like.)*
   HOLY INFANT, SO TENDER AND MILD …
EBENEZER SCROOGE. *(During the above, after a bit.)* It's driving me mad! Faster, faster!
BOB and CHILDREN.
   SLEEP IN HEAVENLY PE-EACE …
BOB. Very, very slow now, children …
BOB and CHILDREN.
   SLEE-EEP IN HEAVENLY PEEEEEEEEEEEEEEEEEACE.
(As the song drags on, Scrooge should feel free to emit noises of enormous frustration — yelps and little screams — as well as to do some angry finger snapping and moving of hands to demand faster tempo.)
EBENEZER SCROOGE. *(During the last notes, he clutches his ears and calls out:)* Make it end, make it end! *(The song finishes.)* Oh thank God.
BOB CRATCHIT. Shall we sing it again, children?
CHILDREN. Oh yes, Father!
EBENEZER SCROOGE. NOOOOOOOOOOO! *(Scrooge rushes at Bob and knocks him off his chair to the ground.)*
GHOST. Mr. Scrooge!
TINY TIM. Father, are you all right?
BOB CRATCHIT. Yes. Something pushed me out of my chair, that's all.
TINY TIM. I hope you're not going to be crippled like me.
BOB CRATCHIT. That's sweet of you to worry, Tiny Tim. You're a sensitive child.
TINY TIM. If we were both crippled, people might not know which one of us to feel sorry for.
CHILD 1. Well then they could feel sorry for both of you.
TINY TIM. That's true. But they might go into sympathetic overdrive, and then start to avoid us.

BOB CRATCHIT. Well, Tiny Tim, it's sweet of you to obsess about it, but really I'm not crippled, I just fell down and went b'm. *(Note: pronounced like boom, but with a shorter vowel sound … somewhere between boom and bum. B'm. The traditional way parents say it to children, but how do you spell that?)*

CHILDREN. *(Delighted.)* B'm! B'm! *(Enter Little Nell. She is a big girl — either tall and big; or even heavy. She carries a large bag [in which she hides some gifts, we will find out]. She's sensitive, like Tiny Tim. But also has a bit of a hale and hearty, "look on the bright side" attitude. So she has energy.)*

LITTLE NELL. Hello, father. Hello, Tiny Tim. Hello, other two children.

BOB CRATCHIT. Look, children, it's your older sister Little Nell, home from the sweatshop. Did you bring home your pitiful salary to help us pay the bills?

LITTLE NELL. I was going to, dearest Father, but then on the street I saw such a pathetic sight. A woman of indeterminate age, shivering in the cold and clutching her starving children. They were weeping and rending their garments. And because it's Christmastime, I felt such a tender feeling in my heart that I just had to give all my salary to them.

BOB CRATCHIT. That's lovely to hear, Little Nell. Children, your sister gives us all a good example.

LITTLE NELL. But I had saved enough money from before, with my nighttime job of selling matches in the snow, that I've been able to buy everyone presents.

TINY TIM. Presents, presents! Oh my little heart may burst!

GHOST. You see how happy and touching they are?

EBENEZER SCROOGE. If you say so. Just promise me they won't sing "Silent Night" again.

LITTLE NELL. Would anyone like to sing "Silent Night" with me?

EBENEZER SCROOGE. NOOOOOOO!!!! *(Scrooge rushes at her and pushes her off her stool. She falls to the ground.)*

LITTLE NELL. Aaaaaaaaaaggghhh! What was that???

GHOST. Mr. Scrooge, stop that!

BOB CRATCHIT. Just a very strong wind in here, darling Little Nell. I like your sweater, is it new?

LITTLE NELL. Yes, Father. I made it myself at the sweatshop from extra yarn and table scraps that fell on the floor. It's my little gift to myself to keep my spirits up.

BOB CRATCHIT. Well it's even nicer than your earlier sweater that your mother made a stew out of. *(Suddenly realizing, worried.)* Children, where is your mother?

TINY TIM. I don't know, Father. We haven't seen her for several hours since she said she was going to jump off the London Bridge.

LITTLE NELL. Oh my gracious.

CHILD 1 and CHILD 2. Mummy, Mummy! We want Mummy!

BOB CRATCHIT. Come, children, let us pray for the safe return of Mrs. Cratchit.

TINY TIM. What if she's dead? Think how pathetic I'll be then!

GHOST. Oh my God, I can't have Mrs. Cratchit be dead. Wait, I'm going to need all my powers. *(The Ghost spreads her arms, with firm authority. Bright light hits her and she intones:)* Hear me, spirits and ghosts around us. By all the powers vested in me from heaven and above, I call upon the forces of the wind and sea to bring Mrs. Bob Cratchit back to her proper home right now! *(Sounds of wind; then nothing.)* Nothing? Okay, what if I do this? *(With a bit of "I hate when I have to stoop to trying this," sings.)* Camptown ladies, sing this song, do da, do da, Camptown races … *(Mrs. Bob Cratchit, her clothes and hair looking wet, comes dancing into the room, suddenly singing the second line along with the Ghost. It's as if the song has magically called her back from the river.)*

MRS. BOB CRATCHIT. *(Singing.)* Camptown races, all day long, oh de do da day! *(Suddenly sees where she is and screams:)* Aaaaaaaaaaaaaaaaggghhh!!!!

GHOST. It worked!

MRS. BOB CRATCHIT. NO NO NO!

CHILDREN. Mummy! Mummy!

TINY TIM. Merry Christmas, Mother. And God bless us, everyone.

MRS. BOB CRATCHIT. No, I don't want to be here.

BOB CRATCHIT. Gladys, are you all right?

MRS. BOB CRATCHIT. Wait a minute. *(She struggles inside her bodice; something is moving around that is bothering her.)* Uh … uh … got it! *(From inside her bodice she brings out a big fish.)* Look children, straight from the filthy, stinking Thames River. Mother's brought home a fish. How'd you all like fish for Christmas dinner?

TINY TIM. No thank you very much. I would prefer a Christmas goose and huckleberries and candied yams and then Mother's special Christmas pudding.

MRS. BOB CRATCHIT. Well you're gonna eat sushi and like it. Here, start nibbling on it now! *(She hands him the fish.)*

EBENEZER SCROOGE. Spirit, why did you bring this woman

back? She clearly was happier at the bottom of the river.

GHOST. Mr. and Mrs. Cratchit are part of the story. They're very poor and they're BOTH very sweet. Now from now on, Mrs. Cratchit will behave correctly. *(Waves her hand toward Mrs. Bob, as if she has power to change her.)*

MRS. BOB CRATCHIT. *(Sweetly.)* Hello, children. Hello, Bob. Hello, Tiny Tim. Mother's home now, Merry Christmas.

LITTLE NELL. Oh look, Mother is her old self again.

MRS. BOB CRATCHIT. *(Sweet.)* That's right, Little Nell. *(Suddenly looks at Little Nell.)* What's that hideous thing you're wearing?

GHOST. Oh dear. Something's wrong with Mrs. Cratchit again. *(Ghost waves her hand again at Mrs. Bob, but Mrs. Bob brushes it away like a mosquito.)*

MRS. BOB CRATCHIT. Little Nell, you stupid child, I've asked you a question.

LITTLE NELL. It's a new sweater I knit for myself at the sweatshop.

MRS. BOB CRATCHIT. You're so awful looking. Haven't I told you repeatedly you look like a bowl of porridge?

LITTLE NELL. When you're the bad mommy you say that. But when you're the good mommy, you stroke my hair and say, "There, there, Little Nell, who cares if you're homely as long as your heart is pure."

MRS. BOB CRATCHIT. Well I'm the bad mommy now. YOU LOOK LIKE A BOWL OF OATMEAL! No one will ever marry you ... or if you did find some sorry soul, he'd pour milk on you, sprinkle sugar on your head, and eat your face for breakfast. *(Little Nell cries.)*

BOB CRATCHIT. Darling, must you continually tell Little Nell she looks like a bowl of oatmeal? She may not be the prettiest flower in the garden, but there's no need to rub her face in it.

MRS. BOB CRATCHIT. And why is she called Little Nell? She's enormous.

LITTLE NELL. Okay, well excuse me for living then. Why don't I just crawl into the gutter and die?

MRS. BOB CRATCHIT. Finally, a constructive suggestion!

EBENEZER SCROOGE. I like Mrs. Cratchit. Is that what I'm supposed to get from seeing this?

GHOST. Oh, God. No it isn't.

MRS. BOB CRATCHIT. Did anyone hear a voice?

BOB CRATCHIT. Your mother is hearing voices, children. We should say a prayer.

MRS. BOB CRATCHIT. *(Somewhat touched.)* I heard a voice saying they liked me. Gosh, I haven't heard anyone say they liked me in a long time. Ever, actually.

TINY TIM. I like you, Mother. I love you.

MRS. BOB CRATCHIT. Oh shut up. You're just hungry. *(Tiny Tim, Little Nell and the two other children weep and cry.)*

BOB CRATCHIT. Gladys, look, you've made the children cry. And on Christmas too.

MRS. BOB CRATCHIT. The children are always crying. Our life is so damnably pathetic. No food to eat, no coal for the stove ... I just hate my life. Does everyone get it?

EBENEZER SCROOGE. She speaks up for herself. It's so unusual.

GHOST. She has a bad attitude.

EBENEZER SCROOGE. Indeed. That's why she's so delightful.

MRS. BOB CRATCHIT. Goodness. I just heard a voice calling me delightful. How unlike the voices I usually hear in my head.

LITTLE NELL. Why does Mother hate us, Father?

MRS. BOB CRATCHIT. Well look in the mirror, why don't you? *(Little Nell weeps.)*

BOB CRATCHIT. Now, now, it's Christmastime. Only happy, loving thoughts and sentences.

TINY TIM. Mummy doesn't hate us. She's just grouchy 'cause she's all wet. I love you, Mummy. My heart is so filled with goodness I can only see your goodness.

MRS. BOB CRATCHIT. Well, isn't that nice?

BOB CRATCHIT. *(Trying to change the subject.)* I have an idea. Maybe it's time for us to open all the Christmas presents that Little Nell has for us. *(Little Nell looks pleased.)*

TINY TIM. Oh yes, may we? Please, please!

CHILD 1 and CHILD 2. Presents, presents!

LITTLE NELL. Ssssssh, not too loud. I didn't have enough money to buy presents for all the children in the root cellar, I don't want them to hear.

TINY TIM. *(Whispers.)* Okay, we'll be quiet.

LITTLE NELL. Father, a present for you. Mother, a present for you. Precious Tiny Tim, a special present for you.

TINY TIM. Oooooooohhhh!

LITTLE NELL. Child One and Child Two, a present each for you. And ... I wish I had another gift to offer to a certain "spirit" I sense in the room.

BOB CRATCHIT. A spirit?

LITTLE NELL. I just had a sense an "otherworldly presence" was here.

TINY TIM. Oooooh, she's scaring me.

BOB CRATCHIT. Now, now, don't be frightened. I don't think there are such things as ghosts and spirits. But you may offer it my present if you like.

LITTLE NELL. I'd like to see if the Ghost would take it from my hand. *(Bob gives Little Nell his present.)*

EBENEZER SCROOGE. Can she see you?

GHOST. I don't think so. It's very confusing. They're not supposed to hear or see me, but it keeps going ka-plooey.

MRS. BOB CRATCHIT. Ka-plooey.

LITTLE NELL. *(Holding out the present.)* Oh Ghost, I'm going to let go of the gift now. If you're there, let me see you catch it and make it float around the room. *(Little Nell lets go of the present. It drops to the floor. Nothing happens.)* Oh. Perhaps no one's there. *(Scrooge mischievously picks up the present and carries it around the room. The Cratchits, one and all, scream.)*

THE CRATCHITS. Aaaaaaaaaaaaaaagggghhhh! *(Scrooge moves the present all over the room in intricate ways. The Cratchits keep screaming. He especially goes out of his way to scare Tiny Tim, keeps waving the present in his face. Finally, annoyed, the Ghost grabs the present from Scrooge.)*

GHOST. Stop that! *(The Ghost throws the present to the ground, and stomps on it repeatedly. The Cratchits stop screaming. Little Nell looks hurt and horrified.)*

LITTLE NELL. Look how it's destroyed the present. Oh, it's so sad.

BOB CRATCHIT. Well that's but one present. I don't need one. And by my count, Little Nell still has presents for the rest of you.

OTHER CHILDREN. Hooray, hooray! *(Tiny Tim, Child 1, Child 2, and Mrs. Bob all receive presents from Little Nell. The children look at theirs in wonderment, they're so prettily wrapped.)*

GHOST. You see how generous Bob Cratchit is? He thinks of others.

MRS. BOB CRATCHIT. "Generous" indeed. He just has this image of himself as noble and good, he's so good out of puffed-up self-regard.

BOB CRATCHIT. What?

MRS. BOB CRATCHIT. Nothing. I'm concentrating on the presents. *(The children start to unwrap their presents. Mrs. Bob weighs hers in her hand.)* Well, it's certainly light enough. What is it, a meringue? *(They all unwrap their presents. Under the festive wrapping, there are cardboard boxes. They open their boxes, and look inside.)*

TINY TIM. They're empty!

CHILD 1. There's nothing in them.

MRS. BOB CRATCHIT. Yes, that's what "empty" means.

LITTLE NELL. I didn't have much money. I spent what I had on the Christmas wrapping.

TINY TIM. *(Disappointed, but covering politely.)* Oh. Well the wrapping was very nice. I wish I hadn't torn it up.

MRS. BOB CRATCHIT. Little Nell. Next time you buy presents, actually buy presents. Don't just give us empty boxes, you idiot child!

LITTLE NELL. I didn't have enough money for presents.

MRS. BOB CRATCHIT. Well then you take the little money you have, and you buy something small and then you DON'T WRAP IT. Or you GIVE us the money directly.

LITTLE NELL. I thought you'd like the wrapping.

MRS. BOB CRATCHIT. Well I didn't!

EBENEZER SCROOGE. Ghost of Christmas Present, why are you showing me this?

GHOST. I don't know. I'm confused.

TINY TIM. Mummy, isn't it time for Christmas dinner? For the Christmas goose and the huckleberries and the candied yams and then the Christmas pudding?

MRS. BOB CRATCHIT. Children, I've been out drinking and trying to drown myself in the Thames — you think I have time to be cooking for you??? God, when will feminism be invented so people won't just assume I'll be cooking all the time, and be positive and pleasant. I wish this were 1977, then I'd be admired for my unpleasantness!

EBENEZER SCROOGE. 1977 sounds interesting. I wonder if they'd like me there too?

GHOST. The two of you are impossible. I don't know how to make you learn the lesson of Christmas. *(Zaps him.)*

EBENEZER SCROOGE. Aaaaaaaagggh! *(The Ghost zaps Mrs. Bob Cratchit.)*

MRS. BOB CRATCHIT. Aaaaaaaaggghhh! *(Looks around accusingly at everyone.)* Who did that? Who did that?

BOB CRATCHIT. Did what, darling?

MRS. BOB CRATCHIT. Somebody did something to my arm.

LITTLE NELL. I thought people would like the wrapping.

BOB CRATCHIT. Now, now, let it go, Little Nell.

TINY TIM. So am I to assume there is no Christmas dinner?

MRS. BOB CRATCHIT. Yes, that's what you're to assume. Why does he talk this way? Is he a British child?

BOB CRATCHIT. Yes, darling, we're all British.

MRS. BOB CRATCHIT. Really? I feel like I'm from Cleveland. Well, never mind. No, Tiny Tim, there's no dinner. We can eat the dust on the floor. *(Child 2 stands, proud to make an announcement.)*

CHILD 2. Mummy, Daddy, Tiny Tim. I have a surprise. While Mummy was in the river, I was in the kitchen — and I cooked the dinner.

THE OTHER CHILDREN. Oooooooooh!!! Christmas dinner!

BOB CRATCHIT. Child Number Two, you're so good. Gladys, maybe it's time we gave him a name.

MRS. BOB CRATCHIT. Okay. *(Names him:)* Martha.

CHILD 2. But I'm a boy.

MRS. BOB CRATCHIT. Okay. Marthum.

CHILD 2. Marthum?

BOB CRATCHIT. It's all right, dear, your mother's difficult, just be glad she called you anything.

MRS. BOB CRATCHIT. That's right. I'm very difficult. But then life is difficult.

BOB CRATCHIT. Gladys, darling. Please look on the bright side once in a while. Our lovely child Marthum has cooked us Christmas dinner. Isn't that nice? Isn't that worth being happy about?

MRS. BOB CRATCHIT. *(Thinks; wants to be negative, but can't think how to spin it bad.)* Yes, but …

BOB CRATCHIT. Yes, but what, darling?

MRS. BOB CRATCHIT. Yes, but … well, I suppose I could be glad about it. It is very nice we can have Christmas dinner, and I didn't have to make it. *(Warning.)* Although I don't want to do dishes afterward.

TINY TIM. I'll do the dishes, precious Mummy.

MRS. BOB CRATCHIT. You always drop the dishes. Although it makes me laugh when you do.

BOB CRATCHIT. Yes, Tiny Tim's so awkward, sometimes it's fun to laugh at him. I mean, with him. *(Tiny Tim smiles happily.)*

MRS. BOB CRATCHIT. All right. I admit it. I'm feeling better. Marthum, thank you for cooking, now perhaps you could go and get the dinner now.

CHILD 2. Can't we sing a song about dinner first?

MRS. BOB CRATCHIT. Oh God, what's all this singing all the

time?

BOB CRATCHIT. It's Christmas, darling. There are carols and hymns and original songs written directly for us, like this next one.

MRS. BOB CRATCHIT. Well all right. I can be in a good mood occasionally.

BOB CRATCHIT. And then after the song, a short intermission so we can use the loo, and then delicious Christmas dinner right after the interval. (Bob, Mrs. Bob, Tiny Tim, Little Nell, and the two other children all sing "The Christmas Dinner Song." It's cheerful and hearty, like a German drinking song, kind of like a celebratory song from Oliver!)

THE CRATCHITS.
   EAT DRINK
   YUMMY YUM YUM
   AT CHRISTMAS EACH YEAR
   WE FILL OUR TUM TUM
   CHEW UP
   AND SAVOR THE MEAL
   AT CHRISTMAS EACH YEAR
   WITH PLEASURE WE SQUEAL

   YAY, YAY, YAY, YAY! ("Yay" rhymes with "say.")
   OUR JOY IS CONTAGIOUS, OUR LAUGHTER
      PROFUSE,
   THE BERRIES AND PUDDING, THE YAMS AND THE
      GOOSE!

   SIP, SLURP
   YUMMY YUM YUM
TINY TIM, CHILD 1 and CHILD 2.
   WE LIKE TO GET DRUNK
   ON EGGNOG AND RUM
THE CRATCHITS.
   CHOW DOWN
   SOME MORSEL OF PORK
LITTLE NELL.
   WE GRAB WITH OUR HANDS
   WE DON'T USE A FORK
THE CRATCHITS.
   YAY, YAY, YAY, YAY!
   IT GETS KIND OF MESSY, THE JELLIES AND JAMS

THE BERRIES AND PUDDING, THE GOOSE AND THE
    YAMS
TINY TIM.
  BLESS US ALL,
  OUR TUMMIES FILL.
  THOUGH I'M SMALL
  MY BELLY WILL
  ACCEPT ALL PIES
  SERVED À LA MODE
  I'LL STUFF THEM DOWN
  'TIL I EXPLODE

(Puffs out his cheeks, indicates stomach exploding. The Ghost prods Scrooge and makes him join the song. So this next section is sung by everyone, the Ghost and Scrooge as well. Mrs. Bob can play she hears additional voices if she wants — though that may be too busy to work.)
EVERYONE.
  GULP, GORGE
  BE GLUTTONOUS TOO
  EACH SWALLOW YOU TAKE
  EACH MOUTHFUL YOU CHEW
  SWIG SWILL
  AND DRINK LOTS OF BEER
  GET DRUNK AND FALL DOWN
  IT'S CHRISTMAS, MY DEAR

  YUM, YUM, YUM, YUM
  WE'RE COVERED WITH GRAVY AND CRANBERRY
    JUICE
  TOO GOOD TO EAT SLOWLY, SO THAT'S OUR
    EXCUSE
  THE BERRIES AND PUDDING, THE YAMS AND THE
    GOOSE!
  YUM YUM!

(The song ends triumphantly. Note: in the last verse, Child 2 might push the dinner in on a big tray with wheels. Director's choice.)

End of Act One

ACT TWO

Scene 10

The Cratchit family is seated around the dinner table. The table has a large swan on it (made of plastic or papier-mâché). The Christmas pudding is very, very large and black and does look like the traditional English Christmas pudding. The Cratchits are frozen in a tableau at the top. The Ghost addresses the audience in a spot. Scrooge stands near her, but is not in the spot. He is not frozen. He's eating a popsicle.

GHOST. *(Sings to audience; a bit sassy.)*
    IF I SHOULD TAKE A NOTION
    TO JUMP INTO THE OCEAN
    T'AIN'T NOBODY'S BUSINESS IF I DO,
    IF I SHOULD GO TO CHURCH ON SUNDAY
    AND "SHIMMY" DOWN ON MONDAY …
(Stops herself.) I guess it really isn't all that Christmasy. Hello. I am still the Ghost of Christmas Present. And we're all in the present, aren't we? I hope you are keeping Christmas well. That you remember to be kind and not make it too commercial, but still support our local stores and help them make a living wage. And that you take sustenance from the touching Cratchit family, so happy even though they only have one good meal a year and are extremely poor. Although maybe their lot will improve if I can change this horrid man's character in the course of this evening. Where did you get that popsicle?
EBENEZER SCROOGE. Someone handed it to me.
GHOST. Bob Cratchit would have given it to one of his children.
EBENEZER SCROOGE. They're about to sit down to an enormous meal. Surely I can have a popsicle.
GHOST. I suppose. *(To audience.)* Now let us watch the Cratchits as they enjoy their Christmas dinner and remember the true meaning of Christmas.

EBENEZER SCROOGE. Why don't you cut your hair off and go buy me something?

GHOST. Be quiet. *(The Cratchit family unfreeze around the table. The Ghost and Scrooge stand apart, watching the Cratchits.)*

THE CHILDREN. Ooooooo, Christmas dinner, Christmas dinner!

TINY TIM. And the goose and the pudding! Oooooh, my little heart may burst.

MRS. BOB CRATCHIT. It looks like a swan. Marthum, is this a swan?

CHILD 2. I don't know. I got it from a lake. I captured it in a big burlap bag, and I beat it senseless with a bat.

LITTLE NELL. A live bat?

CHILD 2. No, a wooden bat.

MRS. BOB CRATCHIT. Well that was very resourceful of you, Marthum.

BOB CRATCHIT. Although normally we like to be kind to animals.

TINY TIM. Just not when we're hungry.

BOB CRATCHIT. That's right, Tiny Tim.

TINY TIM. God bless us, every one!

LITTLE NELL. Father, hurry up and carve the swan, I'm so very hungry. I've only eaten nettles all day. *(Holds up little cloth bag that contains nettles.)*

BOB CRATCHIT. Hmmmmmm, something seems wrong. I can't seem to carve the swan. It's rather tough.

CHILD 2. Did I overcook it?

BOB CRATCHIT. I fear so, Marthum. What little meat was on the swan has been cooked away. There's just skin and bone.

TINY TIM. There's no Christmas goose?

BOB CRATCHIT. Nor Christmas swan neither, it seems.

TINY TIM. Oh. Give me a moment — I must be brave.

CHILD 2. I'm sorry, Mother and Father. I'm sorry, Tiny Tim.

MRS. BOB CRATCHIT. It's inedible. I see. I think we shall no longer call you Marthum. I think we shall call you Useless Child Who Can't Cook.

CHILD 2. Can't I keep the name Marthum?

MRS. BOB CRATCHIT. No you cannot.

BOB CRATCHIT. Darling, Useless Child Who Can't Cook is a very long name. The poor child will be teased ceaselessly in school.

MRS. BOB CRATCHIT. Well maybe she won't go to school. Maybe she'll go straight to the sweatshop like Little Nell.

CHILD 2. Why do you call me "she"? I'm a boy.

MRS. BOB CRATCHIT. Don't tell me what you are. I'll decide, and today I don't know what you are.

CHILD 1. Can I have a name?

MRS. BOB CRATCHIT. No you may not.

TINY TIM. Well at least there's still the Christmas pudding.

THE CRATCHITS. *(Except Mrs. Bob Cratchit.)* Oooooh, the pudding, the pudding. *(Bob spoons the pudding out into little dishes and passes them around. The consistency is of a thick black substance.)*

BOB CRATCHIT. Ohhhh, it's not overcooked. I can scoop it out.

TINY TIM. Oooooh, the pudding, the pudding! *(Bob offers some to Mrs. Bob Cratchit.)*

MRS. BOB CRATCHIT. I'll let you all taste it first. *(The Cratchits start to eat the pudding. They make faces, stick out their tongues, put their dishes back on the tray.)*

THE CRATCHITS. Blllleeeeechhhh! Ehhhhhhyyyyyyyyy!

TINY TIM. It's horrible.

MRS. BOB CRATCHIT. Well of course it's horrible. It's British Christmas pudding. Don't you know what the ingredients are? Rotten fruit and cheap brandy and suet? Don't you know what suet is? It's fat from around animal organs. You think this would make a tasty dish?

TINY TIM. So there's no Christmas dinner, and no Christmas pudding. I can't be brave anymore. *(The Cratchit children cry.)*

MRS. BOB CRATCHIT. This is the very thing I can't stand! All this pathos! It makes me feel hopeless and helpless and I hate it!

EBENEZER SCROOGE. Ghost of Christmas Present, can't we do something?

GHOST. Not without any money.

EBENEZER SCROOGE. I have money. Let me treat them to a Christmas dinner.

GHOST. Really? This is a surprise gesture.

EBENEZER SCROOGE. It's so pathetic, it gets on my nerves. And it wouldn't cost that much to feed them.

GHOST. Okay. *(The Ghost and Scrooge go offstage.)*

TINY TIM. Is there nothing we can eat?

MRS. BOB CRATCHIT. Wait a second. I heard something … let's wait a moment … maybe there will be food.

TINY TIM. Oh dare we hope? Dare we?

MRS. BOB CRATCHIT. Sure, go ahead. *(Scrooge and the Ghost come back, holding many white bags. They also wear little white serving hats. The Cratchits are delighted and amazed.)*

THE CRATCHITS. Ooooooooh. Aaaaaaaaah.

LITTLE NELL. Look how the pretty white bags float through the air.

TINY TIM. It's magic!

GHOST. Here you are, everyone. Happy Meals for everybody. *(The Cratchits each get a white bag and take out French fries and wrapped burgers and sodas.)*

CHILD 1. Ooooooh!!! Hamburgers! French fries!

CHILD 2. Oooooh, the French fries smell delicious.

MRS. BOB CRATCHIT. Well, the French are known for their cooking.

TINY TIM. *(Opening his bag.)* Oooooh, I have a Big Whopper.

MRS. BOB CRATCHIT. Isn't that nice.

TINY TIM. Mummy doesn't have a burger.

MRS. BOB CRATCHIT. Is there a fish fillet?

TINY TIM. No, just burgers.

MRS. BOB CRATCHIT. All right.

LITTLE NELL. At last it feels like true Christmas now. We have our beautiful tree.

MRS. BOB CRATCHIT. Good God! Who decorated the tree?

TINY TIM. I did.

MRS. BOB CRATCHIT. Are you blind as well as crippled?

LITTLE NELL. Mother, please, I'm saying something positive. Now, it feels like a true Christmas. We're all together, and we're happy, and we've exchanged presents, and now we have hamburgers, French fries and colas. Merry Christmas, everyone.

TINY TIM. Merry Christmas, and God bless us everyone!

GHOST. Phew! See?? That's Christmas in the present, and that's poor people taking joy in little things. I hope it's made an impression.

MRS. BOB CRATCHIT. Well all I can say is … *(The Ghost zaps Mrs. Bob Cratchit.)* Aaaaaaaggggghhhhh!

GHOST. I won't have you ruin this happy denouement with one of your sour comments.

MRS. BOB CRATCHIT. All right, all right.

BOB CRATCHIT. Why did you scream, Gladys?

MRS. BOB CRATCHIT. Oh one of those voices … never mind. I screamed because I was so happy. *(Screams again, to "show" that is how she shows happiness.)* Aaaaaaaaaaaggggggghhhh!

BOB CRATCHIT. I'm happy too, darling. *(Makes mild attempt at "happy" scream.)* Aaaaaghh. Merry Christmas, precious Gladys. Merry Christmas, precious children.

CRATCHIT CHILDREN. Merry Christmas, Father, Merry Christmas, Mother. *(Everyone embraces each other, creating a happy tableau. "Scene is over" music.)*

GHOST. Now don't anybody move! *(The Cratchits stay frozen.)* Thank God. *(Throughout the next section, the entire Cratchit family stays frozen in tableau. To Scrooge.)* So your lesson from Christmas Present is over. Now what's still to come is the scarier visit from the Ghost of Christmas Yet to Come. And I warn you, we'll be going to a very scary cemetery.

EBENEZER SCROOGE. Will the Cratchits be part of this? I've really had enough of them. Except for Mrs. Cratchit, of course, I enjoy her.

MRS. BOB CRATCHIT. *(Pleased.)* Oh! How nice. *(Note: From now until further noted, the Cratchits from time to time speak while still staying in tableau.)*

GHOST. It's not up to you to say when you'll see the Cratchits again or not. I feel you're forgetting the seriousness of what we're going through. Plus, I have a feeling Tiny Tim may not be long for this world. And Little Nell may die too.

MRS. BOB CRATCHIT. Tiny Tim may die? And Little Nell too?

TINY TIM. What? This tiny body may be no more?

MRS. BOB CRATCHIT. No, pay no attention, children. Mother is writing a book in her head. Pay no attention.

TINY TIM. You're writing a book about us being dead?

MRS. BOB CRATCHIT. Well, you and Little Nell are so lovable, of course, it would be heartbreaking for a reader to read about you dying.

TINY TIM. Oh thank you, Mummy.

EBENEZER SCROOGE. Oh God, am I going to have to watch these pathetic children's death scenes?

GHOST. Yes, and you're going to like it too.

EBENEZER SCROOGE. You mean, enjoy them?

GHOST. Oh shut up. Come on, go back to your damn chair, sleep a second, and then the Third Spirit will come. Let's get outta here.

EBENEZER SCROOGE. Very well, very well. *(The Ghost and Scrooge exit.)*

MRS. BOB CRATCHIT. Don't go!

BOB CRATCHIT. Gladys, who are you speaking to?

MRS. BOB CRATCHIT. Oh I don't know. I just sensed that those two presences left … and well, one of them, you know, seems to like me. His presence cheers me up.

BOB CRATCHIT. Whose presence, darling?

MRS. BOB CRATCHIT. I don't even know. Never mind. Let's stop standing in this tableau and move around normally, all right? *(They break the tableau, and move normally.)*

BOB CRATCHIT. Children, your mother is hearing voices. We must be very kind.

LITTLE NELL. I hear voices too. I heard the woman's voice say that Tiny Tim and I are going to die.

TINY TIM. Oh dear. And it's true I don't feel very well. I have a feeling I may die.

MRS. BOB CRATCHIT. Nonsense. What would you die of?

TINY TIM. Of being a cripple.

MRS. BOB CRATCHIT. That doesn't make sense. That's like saying you're going to die because you have brown hair.

TINY TIM. Nonetheless I feel it. Unless Mr. Scrooge reforms his personality and learns to value Christmas, I can tell I'm going to die.

MRS. BOB CRATCHIT. What does Mr. Scrooge have to do with it?

BOB CRATCHIT. Oh, Tiny Tim. *(Weeps.)*

MRS. BOB CRATCHIT. He's not dying. He probably feels ill from the Happy Meal, all that fat and grease. Children, if you need to throw up, use one of the white bags the food came in. That's why they put the food in those white bags, it's for vomiting in later on.

TINY TIM. No, it's more serious than throwing up, Mummy.

LITTLE NELL. I feel my mortality too. I have this little bag of nettles still. What if later tonight, I get hungry again and I choke on one of them?

MRS. BOB CRATCHIT. Well you mustn't eat the nettles then.

LITTLE NELL. But if I'm hungry …

MRS. BOB CRATCHIT. Here, give those to me. *(Snatches the little cloth bag full of nettles that Little Nell has carried from before.)* No choking on nettles for you, Young Lady. I've had enough sickness and pathos, and this stupid family where everything is about suffering.

TINY TIM. I think I feel consumption coming on. That's when your little lungs fill up with something and you cough and die, right? *(Coughs poignantly.)*

BOB CRATCHIT. Oh poor Tiny Tim. Other two children, let us pray he doesn't die.

OTHER CHILDREN. Don't die, Tiny Tim, don't die!

MRS. BOB CRATCHIT. *(To Bob.)* Oh why do you encourage him?

LITTLE NELL. He's not the only one dying. The spirit said I was

going to die. Oh, I think I'm starting to choke on an imaginary net-tle. *(Little Nell starts to choke. Tiny Tim keeps coughing softly and poignantly. They both continue to cough and choke during the following:)*
MRS. BOB CRATCHIT. Well, if it's imaginary, how can you choke on it? I've had enough. Wallowing in consumption, poverty, no food, no money, this isn't what I signed up for! It seems like I've walked out on you several times already, but one of these times it's gotta work! So long, everybody — I'm going to the pub and then I'm jumping off the bridge. And don't anyone try to stop me. It's a horrible life.
BOB CRATCHIT. It's a wonderful life.
MRS. BOB CRATCHIT. It isn't! *(Music. The set changes to a pub again. The Cratchit family and set somehow disappear.)*

Scene 11

The Pub. A bartender. Mrs. Bob Cratchit comes storming in.

MRS. BOB CRATCHIT. Give me a Tequila Surprise, and then point me to the river!
BARTENDER. Okay, coming right up. *(Mrs. Bob Cratchit chugs her drink down.)*
MRS. BOB CRATCHIT. Mmmm, delicious! Gimme another! *(Bartender makes her another. Sound of wind begins. Mrs. Bob is pushed about by the wind.)* Oh, it's getting windy! *(More wind sound, music. Enter the Ghost, dressed in black robes, like the figure of Death. She carries a scythe.)*
BARTENDER. Oh my God, it's Death.
MRS. BOB CRATCHIT. Finally! Over here, I'm over here! *(Ebenezer Scrooge follows the Ghost in, momentarily seeming scared.)*
GHOST. Ebenezer Scrooge, behold your gravestone! *(The Ghost points to the ground. Scrooge looks at the floor, sees nothing.)*
EBENEZER SCROOGE. Where?
GHOST. *(Takes off the black hood part of her costume.)* Oh for God's sake. We're not in the cemetery???? Where are we? *(Enter George Bailey, all happy and hyper. Dressed in a 1940s suit.)*
GEORGE BAILEY. My mouth's bleeding, Bert! My mouth …

(Reaches in his pocket.) Zuzu's petals! Zuzu's petals! *(He's in ecstasy finding the flower petals.)* I do exist! Thank you, Clarence. Good old Bedford Falls! It didn't become Pottersville! I've got to go find Mary. Mary, Mary! *(He runs off.)*

EBENEZER SCROOGE. What was that all about?

GHOST. I'm not quite sure. *(The sound of a tinkly bell ringing. Enter a Child.)*

A CHILD. *(In a very sweet, sweet voice.)* Teacher says whenever a bell rings, it's an angel getting its wings. *(George Bailey comes back for a minute.)*

GEORGE BAILEY. That's right, that's right. *(George Bailey and the Child exit.)*

MRS. BOB CRATCHIT. I've never heard that.

GHOST. Me neither. Of course, I'm a Ghost and not an angel. *(Enter Clarence, a sweet, doddering old man of an angel. He has a very large set of wings on his back that make it hard for him to balance.)*

CLARENCE. Well it's true. The bell that just rang was for me — I just got my first pair of wings. Saved that man from killing himself. George Bailey of Bailey Savings and Loan. And now I've got these great big things on me. Ooooh, they make me feel a little unsteady. *(To the Ghost.)* Hello. I'm Clarence. What's your name?

GHOST. My name is Trophenia.

CLARENCE. Trophenia. What a lovely name. I'm an angel, what about you?

GHOST. I'm a ghost.

MRS. BOB CRATCHIT. I hate all this stuff about ghosts and angels. I don't believe it.

CLARENCE. You don't believe your eyes?

MRS. BOB CRATCHIT. I think you're all a piece of undigested mutton. Or a glob of still-fermenting Rice-A-Roni.

EBENEZER SCROOGE. Oh, that's what I said too.

MRS. BOB CRATCHIT. Hello, there. I'm Mrs. Bob Cratchit. Are you Mr. Scrooge?

EBENEZER SCROOGE. Yes. I've enjoyed watching you.

MRS. BOB CRATCHIT. *(Excited.)* Oooooh, watching me do what?

GHOST. *(Notices the flirtation, but focuses back on Clarence.)* Clarence, I wonder if maybe you've been sent to help me. I've tried and tried to make Mr. Scrooge reform himself, but this lady, Mrs. Bob Cratchit, keeps getting in the way with all her negativity. And I try to show him his gravestone, and we end up in a pub.

MRS. BOB CRATCHIT. Well I'd prefer a pub any day.

EBENEZER SCROOGE. Me too. *(They smile at each other.)*

MRS. BOB CRATCHIT. Brilliant minds think alike.

CLARENCE. Well I love to help people, I'm a very good person. Ummm ... let me see. *(To Mrs. Bob Cratchit and Scrooge.)* Which of you two is Mrs. Bob Cratchit?

MRS. BOB CRATCHIT. *(With a look that he's dense.)* Well ... I am.

CLARENCE. I understand you have a bad attitude.

MRS. BOB CRATCHIT. I have a realistic attitude. I'm living in 1840s London, there's no plumbing, everybody smells all the time, I have twenty children — no, twenty-one — or forty-seven, I don't know! — there's never enough food, my husband earns no money cause this man won't pay him anything ...

EBENEZER SCROOGE. Oh, you want me to give him a raise?

MRS. BOB CRATCHIT. *(To Scrooge; flirtatious again.)* No, you're right, he's not worth a raise. You pay him as little as you want. *(Smiles; then back to Clarence.)* It's nonstop pathos in my house. The crippled little boy with innocent little eyes. The big galumphing Little Nell, who eats nettles, whatever they are. *(Waves the bag of nettles in his face.)* And I feel so lonely, and hopeless, and the people around me are icky and goody-goody and pitiful, and I wish I had never been born! *(A little ding noise. Clarence looks focused.)*

CLARENCE. Say that again.

MRS. BOB CRATCHIT. I wish I had never been born! *(The little ding noise again.)*

CLARENCE. Your wish is granted.

MRS. BOB CRATCHIT. What?

CLARENCE. You got it. You've never been born.

MRS. BOB CRATCHIT. Well, nonsense. I'm still here. I'm still holding Little Nell's nettles. *(Reaches for the bag; it's gone.)* Wait. The bag of nettles, where are they?

CLARENCE. You've never been born, so there is no Little Nell. And there's no bag of nettles either. And there is also no Tiny Tim.

GHOST. Excuse me. I don't see how this is going to help. Threatening Scrooge with the death of Tiny Tim is a big part of my strategy.

CLARENCE. Step at a time. This worked with George Bailey, I think it'll work here too. Mrs. Cratchit, or Person X, since you don't exist, you've been granted a great gift. To see what life would've been like if you hadn't been born. Come let's look and see how your husband Bob would be. *(Starts to exit with Mrs. Bob; to Ghost.)* We'll be back in a minute, and I bet she'll be a changed woman.

MRS. BOB CRATCHIT. Wait a minute. I want Mr. Scrooge to come along, for moral support.

EBENEZER SCROOGE. I'd be happy to, fine lady. *(Flirtatious.)* And you are a fine lady.

GHOST. I'm so thrown. Nowhere in the story does Scrooge fall in love with Mrs. Bob Cratchit.

EBENEZER SCROOGE. I'm not in love … *(With a smile to Mrs. Bob Cratchit.)* … yet. I'm just flirting. *(The Ghost looks a little alarmed by this interest from Scrooge.)*

CLARENCE. Now, now, don't lose faith. Come with me, and we'll see what would've happened had Gladys Cratchit never been born. *(The pub goes away. We're back at the Cratchits' house.)*

Scene 12

The Cratchit house. Sad music. Bob Cratchit is seated, crying, wiping his eye with a handkerchief. Seated on the ground are Child 1 and Child 2. Mrs. Cratchit, Scrooge, Clarence and the Ghost are there too, invisible, and they watch.

GHOST. Oh, he's crying. Awwwwww.

CHILD 1. Father? Why are you crying?

BOB CRATCHIT. It's nothing. *(Weeps some more.)*

CHILD 1. Are you sad?

BOB CRATCHIT. No, children.

CHILD 2. I hope you're not sad, Father.

BOB CRATCHIT. It's sweet of you to worry, Little Molly and Little Willie.

MRS. BOB CRATCHIT. That's not their names. They didn't have names.

CLARENCE. With you not there, they were given names.

MRS. BOB CRATCHIT. Well bully for them.

BOB CRATCHIT. I'm not crying because I'm sad, children. I'm crying because I'm happy.

CHILD 2. You are?

BOB CRATCHIT. Yes, Little Willie.

MRS. BOB CRATCHIT. I would never call a child Little Willie.

BOB CRATCHIT. Sometimes you cry when you're happy because the thing you're happy about has touched a tender place in your heart.

MRS. BOB CRATCHIT. I just hate this man. He's so superior in all his suffering. Does anyone else see it?

EBENEZER SCROOGE. I certainly do.

CHILD 1. Oh, Father, does this mean Mother is bringing home another child?

BOB CRATCHIT. Yes, she's promised she would. Dear Mrs. Cratchit.

MRS. BOB CRATCHIT. I thought I didn't exist.

CLARENCE. Be quiet, please, pay attention.

BOB CRATCHIT. Here she comes now. *(Enter Bob's wife. Let's call her The Nice Mrs. Cratchit. She's lovely, sweet, calm, generous. She's perfection. She even speaks beautifully. She's carrying a little bundle, wrapped up.)*

THE NICE MRS. CRATCHIT. Hello, Bob, darling. Hello, Little Willie, Little Tom. I have a wonderful surprise for you all.

BOB CRATCHIT. Dare I hope? Is it another child?

THE NICE MRS. CRATCHIT. Yes, I found a foundling on the steps of the church today. Father Meghan M'Golly said he would give it to the Catholic orphanage, but I said, no, Father, Bob and I so love children, no matter how little money we have, there's always room for another little one.

BOB CRATCHIT. Oh, Mrs. Cratchit. How I love you. You're so wonderful and good.

THE NICE MRS. CRATCHIT. And so are you, Bob. The goodness in your heart makes me feel so warm that we don't even need those odd energy units you bought from Mr. Scrooge and Kenneth Lay.

BOB CRATCHIT. Mr. Scrooge? Who's that?

THE NICE MRS. CRATCHIT. Oh I'm sorry. I think he doesn't exist. I mean from your boss, Mr. Lay.

EBENEZER SCROOGE. I don't exist either? I don't understand.

GHOST. *(To Clarence.)* Please, he's the leading character in the work I'm supposed to be doing.

CLARENCE. Oh, sorry, I somehow made both of them not exist. How did I do that?

BOB CRATCHIT. Yes, Meredith, I'm going to get a lawyer, and look into these energy units. They feel bogus to me.

THE NICE MRS. CRATCHIT. Oh Bob, you're so bright as well as loving. Yes, let's go to the law firm of Havisham, Heap and Fagin, and sue the pants off them.

BOB CRATCHIT. I will have justice. I won't just lie down and take it.

MRS. BOB CRATCHIT. Bob would never say that.

CLARENCE. Maybe with you not born he would.

BOB CRATCHIT. But I'm forgetting this bundle of joy. Let me look at it. Oh what an adorable child. Hee haw, hee haw. Oh. I felt a sudden pang of missing the children in the root cellar.

THE NICE MRS. CRATCHIT. Now, Bob, we both agreed … it was too small for them down there. And we found them a wonderful home, and we didn't have to split them up, Mia Farrow took all eighteen of them.

BOB CRATCHIT. Sill I do miss them.

THE NICE MRS. CRATCHIT. Oh you're so tender-hearted. That's why I love you, Bob Cratchit. But let's focus on the new baby, Hee Haw.

BOB CRATCHIT. What?

THE NICE MRS. CRATCHIT. Didn't you name the child Hee Haw?

BOB CRATCHIT. No, no, I just said that, you know like baby talk. Googie-googie.

THE NICE MRS. CRATCHIT. I think Hee Haw is a better name than Googie-googie.

MRS. BOB CRATCHIT. Oh she's an idiot.

THE NICE MRS. CRATCHIT. Well, we'll name the baby later on. Now, say! Where's Fido? Shouldn't he meet the new addition too?

BOB CRATCHIT. Yes, where is that dog? Oh, Fido! *(Enter Tiny Tim on all fours, barking and panting.)* Look, Fido, a new bundle of joy in the family. *(Tiny Tim barks approvingly.)*

THE NICE MRS. CRATCHIT. What a good and loving dog he is. And so good with children.

MRS. BOB CRATCHIT. I don't understand, what's this?

CLARENCE. Well you weren't born, so the soul of Tiny Tim incarnated into a dog.

MRS. BOB CRATCHIT. Really? *(Laughs.)* I'm oddly amused. Well I don't see him limping. He's not a cripped dog?

THE NICE MRS. CRATCHIT. How's Fido's paw today?

BOB CRATCHIT. Oh much better. And I taught him to roll over and play dead. Roll over, Fido! *(Tiny Tim rolls over.)* Very good. Now play dead. *(Tiny Tim lies down still.)* Good boy. Now, where's Flicka?

Oh, Flicka! *(Little Nell comes bounding into the room. She is a horse.)*
LITTLE NELL. Neigh!!!!! Neigh!!!!!!! *(Shakes her mane, stomps her foot.)*
BOB CRATCHIT. Flicka, my friend Flicka — look, a new baby.
LITTLE NELL. Neigh!!!!!
MRS. BOB CRATCHIT. Little Nell is a horse? Well that's fine. Tell me, does she eventually get turned into glue?
THE NICE MRS. CRATCHIT. Bob, I know you love little Flicka. But I've been meaning to speak to you about having her in the house. *(Nell/Flicka looks mad, snorts, stomps.)* Granted she's a wonderful horse, but she's so big, and she always bumps into the walls and the furniture.
BOB CRATCHIT. I know, Meredith dear. But I feel such a tender feeling in my heart for both Tiny Fido and Little Flicka.
THE NICE MRS. CRATCHIT. Well maybe someday we can afford a stable. *(Nell/Flicka doesn't like this conversation, and neighs and whinnies and stamps a bit.)*
BOB CRATCHIT. There, there, little Flicka, we won't put you in the stable, I promise. Oh Tiny Fido, you can stop playing dead now. *(Tiny Tim gets up, pants and barks happily. He now kneels, pants and does a dog's "begging for food" gesture.)* Oh Meredith, darling, I think Tiny Fido and the children are hungry.
THE NICE MRS. CRATCHIT. Well, no worry — I have a delicious, elaborate, carefully prepared Christmas dinner simmering in the kitchen. Christmas goose, huckleberries, candied yams and the pièce de résistance, pudding. And don't worry, children, it's just tapioca — no rotted fruit, no suet, just lovely eggy goodness and those little tapioca things all through it.
CHILDREN. Ooooooh, Mummy! Scrumptious! *(Tiny Tim and Little Nell/Flicka bark and neigh and show their approval too. The Nice Mrs. Cratchit exits to the kitchen.)*
CHILD 2. Oh, Daddy — Mummy is the best mummy in the world.
BOB CRATCHIT. Yes, she is, Little Willie. The best mummy and the best wife in all of Christendom. She is perfection.
CLARENCE. You see, Mrs. Cratchit — what life would have been like if you had never been born? *(Mrs. Bob Cratchit is a bit speechless.)*
MRS. BOB CRATCHIT. Well, yeah. She's perfection, and I was a disaster. So everyone's much happier with me never having been born. *(There is a pause.)*
CLARENCE. Well … um …
EBENEZER SCROOGE. She's right. Bob Cratchit seems happier.

And he has some energy, and he wants to sue people.

MRS. BOB CRATCHIT. And this other Mrs. Cratchit is much nicer than I ever was. They're compatible, they seem to like each other, they both love foundlings. She's a good cook apparently.

CLARENCE. Yes, but Tiny Tim and Little Nell …

MRS. BOB CRATCHIT. Well, Tiny Tim and Little Nell seem happy as a dog and a horse. He doesn't limp, she doesn't work in a sweatshop, she doesn't look like oatmeal as much as she did. They seem fine to me. I mean, I was just going to kill myself, but now I agree with you — I should just never have existed, that's much the better thing.

CLARENCE. Yes, but …

MRS. BOB CRATCHIT. No, let's just leave it as it is — I've never existed.

CLARENCE. Well, um … uh … um … uh …

GHOST. Well, thanks a lot, Clarence! Thanks to you, Mrs. Cratchit is HAPPY not existing; and Mr. Scrooge hasn't learned anything and he somehow doesn't exist.

CLARENCE. Now, now, stay calm. Maybe I can get some guidance from Tess or Monica.

GHOST. From who?

CLARENCE. You don't know Tess and Monica? Have you never been touched by an angel? Used to be on CBS Sunday nights, now you can see it on the Pax Channel?

GHOST. I just watch World Wide Wrestling and the Weather Channel.

CLARENCE. Well, Monica is the lovely Irish angel, and Tess is the older angel who sings gospel, and each week they solve people's lives in under an hour.

GHOST. Do you think Monica and Tess could help us?

CLARENCE. Well, Mrs. Cratchit didn't react like George Bailey, so I need help from someone, I'm just this doddering old man with wings. Here, let me try. Tess! Monica! Tess! Monica! (A lovely brunette woman with long hair and a tasteful blouse and skirt shows up in a balcony. We can see her, but the characters can't. I call her Lovely Irish Voice. An alternate way is to have her only on the sound system. But seeing her is probably better.)

LOVELY IRISH VOICE. (With a lovely Irish lilt.) Yes, Clarence?

CLARENCE. Oh, Monica. How lovely to hear your lilting voice.

LOVELY IRISH VOICE. Thank you, Clarence. Congratulations on your wings. You look fine in them. Tess and I are planning to invite you to a nice vacation in Bermuda to celebrate.

CLARENCE. Oh that's very kind of you. Now, the reason I was calling you is … well, things worked out fine with George Bailey, but I'm afraid Mrs. Bob Cratchit has decided she *likes* not existing.

MRS. BOB CRATCHIT. I do. I love it. I don't exist, I don't exist! No children, no headaches. I get to sleep 'til noon. Eat bonbons, read mystery novels. It's my kind of life — no life at all.

LOVELY IRISH VOICE. Oh, my. Oh heavens to Betsy. What shall we do? Let me confer with Tess a moment. Tess, oh, Tess … *(Lovely Irish Voice leaves her balcony, or pokes her head offstage. We don't see who she speaks with, only hear her. The woman's voice we hear is meant to be Tess, Della Reese on* Touched by an Angel. *Not looking for an imitation, just a low, melodious voice. And when she speaks, it's an in-the-distance mumble that we can only hear certain words of.)*

WOMAN'S VOICE. *(Singing to herself, muffled low voice.)* Amazing grace, how sweet the sound …

LOVELY IRISH VOICE. Tess, can I confer with you a moment? *(The sound of Monica and the woman Tess conferring, in muffled tones, distant. We can't hear what they're saying. We hear the two voices mumble back and forth. Occasionally we hear a word in the midst of the mumbling — probably in the lower timbre of Tess's voice.*

LOVELY IRISH VOICE and TESS'S VOICE. *(Mostly muffled, we hear occasional word.)* bzzzz bzzzzz bzzzzz bzzzzzzz God bzzzzzz bzzzzzz bzzzzzzz bzzzzzzz state o' grace bzzzzzzzzzz bzzzzzzzzz bzzzzzzzzz glory be bzzzzzzzzzzzz bzzzzzzzzzzz. *(Everyone listens attentively to this voice.)*

MRS. BOB CRATCHIT. Gosh, it's turned into a radio play.

LOVELY IRISH VOICE and TESS'S VOICE. bzzzzzzzz bzzzzzzzzz heaven bzzzzzzzzzzzz bzzzzzzzz Scrooge Mrs. Cratchit bzzzzzz bzzzzzz warm milk. *(The conference appears to be over. Lovely Irish Voice returns to her balcony.)*

LOVELY IRISH VOICE. Clarence, I have good news. Tess and I looked in the heavenly files, and Mrs. Cratchit and Mr. Scrooge are in the wrong century. So you were right to take her out of 1840s London, Mr. Cratchit is meant to be with the second Mrs. Cratchit, not the first.

CLARENCE. And Tiny Tim and Little Nell are meant to be a dog and a pony?

LOVELY IRISH VOICE. Ummmm … well I know that doesn't sound right, and we forgot to check on them, but Meredith Cratchit is definitely the correct Mrs. Cratchit. And the Mrs. Cratchit who presently doesn't exist is meant to be married to Mr.

Scrooge, and they're meant to live in New York City in 1977. *(Mrs. Bob Cratchit and Scrooge look at one another, startled.)*

CLARENCE. I see. How do we make that happen? *(Special spot on Lovely Irish Voice and on Clarence only. Note: Scrooge and Mrs. Bob sneak offstage in darkness. Or if seen, exit with a "how very strange this news is" look on their faces.)*

LOVELY IRISH VOICE. Well, let's see. Little Nell the horse should stamp its hoof ten times. Then you and the Ghost of Christmas Yet to Come should say the phrase "Silly Sally Sat with Sibyl Setting Spells and Seeking Secret Shadows, Spooks and Specters." You should say it ten times. And then there should be music, lights and set change. *(The Lovely Irish Voice disappears. In a spotlight Little Nell starts to stamp her hoof ten times, saying "Neigh" on each stamp. Then Clarence and the Ghost come into a spot, and while Little Nell continues, they intone:)*

CLARENCE and GHOST. Silly Sally Sat with Sibyl Setting Spells and Seeking Secret Shadows, Spooks and Specters.

Silly Sally sat with Sibyl Setting Spells and Seeking Secret Shadows, Spooks and Specters.

Silly Sally Sat with Sibyl Setting Spells and Seeking Secret Shadows, Spooks and Specters. *(Etc. for ten times; if they have trouble saying it, or get the giggles, that's fine. Fewer than ten times is fine if set is ready.)*

Scene 13

A fancy living room. Modern, nouveau riche furniture, at least a few touches. A big fancy Christmas tree, white, with silver and gold decorations. Mrs. Bob Cratchit comes into the room, admiring a ring on her hand. She is all dolled up, has a very modern, piled-on-her head hairdo. She looks good actually.

MRS. BOB CRATCHIT. Oh what a beautiful ring. I just love it. 3,455 carats — it's marvellous. Harry, darling — I love it, thank you. *(Ebenezer Scrooge comes in, dressed in a fancy satin dressing gown over slacks and shirt. He uses a walker but otherwise seems fairly healthy.)*

EBENEZER SCROOGE. What? What did you say?

MRS. BOB CRATCHIT. I said, I love my new present. It's marvelous, Harry. And this is so much better than 1840s London.

EBENEZER SCROOGE. Well, I'm glad you like it, darling. But you called me Harry again.

MRS. BOB CRATCHIT. Ebenezer, dear, I told you, I've changed our names. I don't want to be reminded of whatever that awful other life was. Now your name is Harry, and my name is Leona. And we're the toast of the town, and I eat bonbons all morning, and then in the afternoon I supervise the staff in all your hotels. And, Harry darling, I love my new ring. It's simply marvelous.

EBENEZER SCROOGE. Well I'm glad you like it ... "Leona." *(Twitches slightly.)* Bah humbug! Kaplooey! *(Back to normal.)* Sorry, darling. Just my old Tourette's acting up. Now, Leona, one of our hotels just called up, and said you fired the chief housekeeper.

MRS. BOB CRATCHIT. Yes, I did. I didn't like the way she looked at me.

EBENEZER SCROOGE. How did she look at you?

MRS. BOB CRATCHIT. She looked at me sideways. Like this. *(Shows a look, looking sideways, eyes narrowed.)*

EBENEZER SCROOGE. Well whatever you think is best. I remember what fun it was to be mean to Bob Cratchit.

MRS. BOB CRATCHIT. *(Quivers.)* Please don't mention that terrible name to me.

EBENEZER SCROOGE. Well I'm glad you fired the housekeeper and I hope you enjoyed it.

MRS. BOB CRATCHIT. Thank you, I did. *(He kisses her.)* Don't mess the hair.

EBENEZER SCROOGE. I find you so exciting. You're so mean. Do something mean, let me watch.

MRS. BOB CRATCHIT. Okay. Serena! Serena! *(Enter a downtrodden maid, Serena.)*

SERENA. Yes, Mrs. Helmsley?

MRS. BOB CRATCHIT. Did you finish scrubbing the bathroom?

SERENA. Yes. It was hard to get the smell out.

MRS. BOB CRATCHIT. Well, Harry's old, what can I say? Serena ... did you dust in here?

SERENA. Oh yes, Mrs. Helmsley.

MRS. BOB CRATCHIT. What about the floor?

SERENA. I dusted the floor.

MRS. BOB CRATCHIT. Did you dust under it?

SERENA. Under it? I dusted ... the floor.

MRS. BOB CRATCHIT. I asked if you dusted UNDER it.

SERENA. What do you mean?

MRS. BOB CRATCHIT. Did you lift up the floorboards and dust UNDER it? Yes or no?

SERENA. No. But it would be too heavy to lift up the floorboards.

MRS. BOB CRATCHIT. Well maybe I need a maid on steroids who can lift things better. Is that what I should get, Serena?

SERENA. I'm sorry, Mrs. Helmsley, wait, let me try to lift up the floorboards now. *(Kneels down, tries to lift floor; Scrooge and Mrs. Bob enjoy this a lot.)* Uhhhhhh. Uhhhhhhh. I think I need a screwdriver.

MRS. BOB CRATCHIT. It's too late, Serena. You're fired.

SERENA. What?

MRS. BOB CRATCHIT. I said you're fired.

SERENA. But it's Christmas Eve! I have four children.

MRS. BOB CRATCHIT. Christmas means nothing to me. You're fired, get out, get out!

SERENA. Oh! It's Christmas, I'm going to starve! *(She runs out weeping.)*

MRS. BOB CRATCHIT. You're one of the little people!

EBENEZER SCROOGE. Leona, that was delightful. I love you!

MRS. BOB CRATCHIT. Thank you, Harry. And I love you, and I love your money and the jewels you give me. Money, status, physical things. That's what I value in life.

EBENEZER SCROOGE. That's what I value too. Bah humbug!

MRS. BOB CRATCHIT. Oh Tourette's again?

EBENEZER SCROOGE. No, that time I said it for real. Bah humbug on everything except money.

MRS. BOB CRATCHIT. Harry, buy me another hotel!

EBENEZER SCROOGE. You got it, baby! *(Scrooge and Mrs. Bob Cratchit embrace. Enter the Ghost, now with wings.)*

GHOST. Well, as you see. I got my wings, whatever that means. *(Frowns, discombobulated.)* So we've gotten Scrooge and Mrs. Cratchit into the right century. And Bob and the other Mrs. Cratchit are pretty happy back in the 1840s. And so, um … *(Frowns again.)* … well the moral of the story confuses me sort of. But there must be one, it all feels sort of right. Let's see. The moral is there are some people who are mean and nasty, but if they enjoy being mean and nasty, then they're happy. That's moral number one. Doesn't sound too good, does it? I bet if I phrased it another way, it would be better. "If you have money, you might as well enjoy it." Maybe that's the moral, I don't know. Moral number two … *(Bob Cratchit, The Nice Mrs. Cratchit, Tiny Tim the dog and Little Nell the horse, and Child 1 and*

Child 2 come out.) … is that there are other people who are very sweet and nice and are just lovely people. And even when they're poor, they're happy. And the mean people can only be happy when they're rich. So the moral is, "If you're poor, you can be happy; and if you're mean, you better get money." *(Shrugs.)* I'm sorry if that doesn't sound uplifting, but the story doesn't make sense to me anymore. Although Clarence and I are about to join Tess and Monica in Bermuda. Maybe after a rest I'll understand it all better. And now … *(Waves her zapper like a wand; music introduction.)* … a Christmas blessing from Bob and Meredith Cratchit and their children, dog and horse. *(Ghost moves to the side and watches the Cratchits sing.)*

BOB and NICE MRS. CRATCHIT.
WE'RE SO HAPPY AND WE'RE POOR
ROOF MAY LEAK BUT WE IGNORE
ALL THE TROUBLES WE MAY SEE
'CAUSE WE'RE FILLED WITH GAIETY
HIP HOORAY AND YUP-DE-DOO
WE FEEL HAPPY THROUGH AND THROUGH
THOUGH WE'RE POOR WE HAVE SUCH FUN
SO GOD BLESS US EVERYONE
FA LA LA LA LA LA LA LA!

(Tiny Tim barks happily. Enter Scrooge and Mrs. Bob Cratchit.)
SCROOGE and MRS. BOB CRATCHIT.
WE'RE SO HAPPY 'CAUSE WE'RE RICH
MRS. BOB CRATCHIT.
I'M SHORT-TEMPERED, I'M A BITCH
SCROOGE.
STILL I LOVE THAT SHE'S SO MEAN
MRS. BOB CRATCHIT.
AND HIS MONEY IS QUITE GREEN
SCROOGE and MRS. BOB CRATCHIT.
EXCESS WEALTH IS WHAT WE LOVE
TO SUCCEED YOU PUSH AND SHOVE
SO IF POOR FOLK FALL BEHIND
WE CAN'T SAY WE REALLY MIND!

(The Ghost comes forward.)
GHOST.
THE MORAL OF THE STORY
CONFUSES ME TONIGHT
NASTY PEOPLE TRIUMPH
NO THAT CAN'T BE RIGHT

(Enter Clarence.)

CLARENCE.
   THE MORAL OF THE STORY
   IT'S BEST THAT YOU BE POOR
   AND LEAVE IT TO THE ANGELS
   TO EVEN UP THE SCORE

(Ghost and Clarence zap Scrooge and Mrs. Bob Cratchit.)

SCROOGE and MRS. BOB CRATCHIT. Ow! Ow!

BOB and HIS FAMILY.
   WHAT IS CHRISTMAS AT ITS CORE
   GIVING COMFORT TO THE POOR

MRS. BOB CRATCHIT. *(Pointing toward the Cratchits.)*
   I'M SO GLAD THAT I'M NOT THERE
   AND I LOVE MY BRAND-NEW HAIR

EVERYONE.
   MERRY CHRISTMAS WHOOP-DE-DOO
   WE FEEL HAPPY THROUGH AND THROUGH
   RICH MAN, POOR MAN, SAID AND DONE
   SO GOD BLESS US EVERYONE

BOB and HIS FAMILY.
   LOVE YOUR NEIGHBOR, HELP HIM THRIVE

MRS. BOB CRATCHIT. More for me, more for me!

BOB and HIS FAMILY.
   HONEST LABOR, NINE TO FIVE

MRS. BOB CRATCHIT. Give me money for nothing, money for nothing!

BOB and HIS FAMILY.
   AND AT CHRISTMAS PLEASE BELIEVE

MRS. BOB CRATCHIT. More diamonds, Harry!

SCROOGE. All right, sweetie.

BOB and HIS FAMILY.
   BETTER GIVE THAN TO RECEIVE
   LA LA LA LA LA LA LA

(Etc. They sing "la la la" under next dialogue.)

MRS. BOB CRATCHIT. Who are these people singing, Harry?

SCROOGE. I don't know. I'm going senile.

MRS. BOB CRATCHIT. Do I have power of attorney?

SCROOGE. Yes, darling, you get to say yes or no on everything.

MRS. BOB CRATCHIT. Oh, Ebenezer.

SCROOGE. Oh, Gladys. Look, I bought you a zillion-dollar tiara. Bah humbug!

MRS. BOB CRATCHIT. Bah humbug to you too, Harry. *(Puts it on.)* Oh, Harry. I feel like a queen. *(Big musical windup. Everyone does a showbizzy choreographed final verse, with Scrooge and Mrs. Bob down front.)*
EVERYONE.
   WHAT IS CHRISTMAS, WHAT'S IT FOR?
   FOR THE RICH OR FOR THE POOR?
   IT'S FOR BOTH, YOU SILLY GUS
   IT'S FOR YOU AND ME AND US
   MERRY CHRISTMAS WHOOP-DE-DOO
   THOUGH THE MORAL SEEMS ASKEW
   STILL THE TALE THAT HAS BEEN SPUN
   ENDS GOD BLESS US EVERY, EVERYONE!
(Everyone in their way seems very happy.)

End of Play

PROPERTY LIST

Toys
Christmas tree
Punch bowl, ladle
Tiny Christmas tree
Plastic or papier-mâché swan
Christmas pudding
White Christmas tree
Crutch (TINY TIM)
Pen, notebook (BOB CRATCHIT)
Printed list (SCROOGE)
Two wrapped packages (GHOST)
Electrical zapper (GHOST)
White gym socks (GHOST)
Needlepoint (MRS. BOB CRATCHIT)
Bundle wrapped in blanket (BOB CRATCHIT,
    NICE MRS. CRATCHIT)
Bottle of liquor, glass (BARTENDER)
Glass of punch (MRS. BOB CRATCHIT)
Pot of porridge and ladle (BEADLE, BEADLE'S WIFE)
Bowls and spoons (YOUNG JACOB, YOUNG EBENEZER)
Removable beard (GHOST)
Watch fob (MRS. DUTCH PERSON)
Comb (MR. DUTCH PERSON)
Bag with gifts (LITTLE NELL)
Fish (MRS. BOB CRATCHIT)
Wheeled dinner tray (CHILD)
Popsicle (SCROOGE)
Cloth bag with nettles (LITTLE NELL)
Spoons, pudding dishes (BOB CRATCHIT)
White serving hats (SCROOGE, GHOST)
White bags with French fries, burgers, and sodas
    (SCROOGE, GHOST)
Scythe (GHOST)
Flower petals (GEORGE BAILEY)
Handkerchief (BOB CRATCHIT)
Walker (SCROOGE)

SOUND EFFECTS

Wailing of ghosts
Clock striking one
Zapping
Air rustling
Popping
Noise and commotion
Clock striking two
Wind
Bell ringing

AFTERWORD

I was asked by Tracy Brigden, artistic director of City Theatre in Pittsburgh, to write a comic alternative Christmas play. I knew and liked Tracy from when she worked at Manhattan Theatre Club, and also directed around New York City.

I wasn't sure what topic I was going to choose, and I was looking around at the various Christmas literature. Dickens' *A Christmas Carol* and Frank Capra's 1946 film *It's a Wonderful Life* seemed the two most dominant Christmas stories. And, of course, many regional theatres present *A Christmas Carol* every year; and the television has been airing *It's a Wonderful Life* every year as well.

I had seen *A Christmas Carol* many times, especially the various movie versions. My favorite, like many, is the British 1951 version starring the fabulous Alastair Sims. I had never read the actual Dickens story and finally did so. It's quite good … though I found out that one of my favorite scenes in the 1951 British film is not in the story (and thus is an invention of the screenwriter, though a most logical one) — it's Scrooge's sweet and eloquently simple apology to his nephew's wife for all his years of ignoring them.

Anyway, somewhere in the midst of relooking at the Dickens story, I suddenly wondered what would happen if Mrs. Bob Cratchit — who is barely in the story or in the movies, but merely exists as a stoic, "good" mother and wife, who bears all the family's suffering with never a complaint — just hated her life and wanted out.

I love the writing of Dickens, but it's also true his Good Characters can be on the goody-goody side. And so the impulse behind this play was to have this super-modern, super-not-good-sport, super-fed-up Mrs. Cratchit plopped down in the play.

*****

I've found that some audience members who like my darker, more satiric work (like *Sister Mary Ignatius Explains It All for You* or *Betty's Summer Vacation*) can be frustrated when they see lighter work of mine, like this play or like *The Actor's Nightmare*.

Satire usually has a sting and a bit of purpose — it's usually critical of some aspect of life or an institution or a government. *Sister Mary* is critical of some Catholic dogma (for its rigidity sometimes, for its illogic sometimes); while *Betty's Summer Vacation* is critical of our fascination with tabloid sleaze (those fascinating but disgusting court cases we get hooked on that show the worst side of human nature).

Parody is friendlier, less pointed, and doesn't really have any purpose beyond entertaining — and entertaining partially by playing free and fast with what we know about certain works. For instance, I adore the plays of Tennessee Williams, including *The Glass Menagerie*. I was so happy that critics mostly referred to my parody of it — *For Whom the Southern Belle Tolls* — as a "fond parody." Because it was.

So this play too is a parody and mostly a fond one. I like *A Christmas Carol.* I maybe don't want to see it 103 times. But I think it's a sweet and moving parable. So I don't have a satiric purpose of "I hate Christmas stories." Instead it's to play with the Christmas sentimentality by mixing it up all together — with bits of O. Henry's *Gift of the Magi* and the film *It's a Wonderful Life* and with *Oliver Twist* thrown in for good measure.

And it's a kind of "what if" story — what if there was a rebel in the midst of *A Christmas Carol*, a Mrs. Cratchit who hated the suffering of her life and railed against it, and tried to escape it. And that "what if" throws the story out of whack, so that Scrooge instead of learning his "good lesson" learns instead to admire Mrs. Cratchit's orneriness; and the Ghost at the end is forced to try to find a moral in something that no longer quite makes sense to her.

So this isn't one of my dark plays. And you might consider communicating that to your audiences (if you think it's a good idea to do so).

*****

Now as to production and/or acting issues. When I write these notes, I base the suggestions on things I've learned from productions and sometimes from auditions.

I've had less experience with this play than with other plays I've written notes for. I've only been involved in the one production — the excellent one at City Theatre. I was involved with the casting of Mrs. Bob, Scrooge and the Ghost, but was not able to be involved in the casting of the other roles. (I, by the way, was very impressed with the actors who did the play in Pittsburgh — all 12 of them. 14, counting the two children who doubled.)

So my advice will be a little less informed than it might have been. I also worry that the play is a bit too long ... I have an idea that with a couple of other productions under my belt, I'd know where to make cuts. The City Theatre production had such a good pace to it that no one section called out to be cut. But still I'm aware that it's a bit long. So keep aware of having a quick pace to the acting, and be careful of scene changes happening quickly and smoothly if possible.

So here are some of the issues I've noticed.

The Ghost. At the beginning, she's the welcoming hostess — gracious, friendly, etc. When she gets irritated with the children for her various reasons, go there ... but don't hold on to it during the speeches where the children are not being mentioned. One of the traps is to make the whole opening be about her irritation with children ... and it should only be a small part. Mostly she should be welcoming the audience and telling the story. Oh — and January Murelli, who was terrific in the part, also added an occasional Lena Horne-ish sass to her voice on certain lines (such as "he was a nasty little child").

The set. At City Theatre we chose to have the set look much like a "regular" set for *A Christmas Carol*. Since that play (and mine) have lots of different scenes, having full sets for each place is cumbersome and expensive. So the set was a pretty, purposely generic backdrop of old London, and either furniture pieces or partial walls and furniture were all that was added, as needed.

Little Nell is one of Dickens' most famous pathetic good children. Pauline Kael quoted someone (I forget whom) as saying they could never trust anyone who didn't laugh at the death of Little Nell. So I decided to add her (from the not-that-read-anymore *The Old*

Curiosity Shop), so that cranky Mrs. Cratchit had to deal with not only pathetic Tiny Tim but also Little Nell. However, in the writing of the part, she took on another color, one the actress at City Theatre, Sheila McKenna, took on beautifully: Instead of simpering sensitivity, she had a brave, "hale and hearty," upbeat energy, as if she always looked on the bright side and tried to get everyone else to do so too. That's a very good thing to play, and I think is also great for keeping the pace up.

The eating/drinking song that ends ACT ONE — is meant to be rousing and upbeat. The movie *Oliver* has very much the kind of emphatic musical staging I was thinking of. (And that movie's staging is somewhat parodied in the Monty Python film *The Meaning of Life,* especially in the "Every Sperm is Sacred" song.) So the staging is mostly swaying back and forth but with great commitment and happiness. Any other staging could and should be "traditional" and satisfying in that old-fashioned, predictable way. Hoping that makes sense.

Accents. I mean for almost all of the actors to have British accents — and very conventional, "easy" accents are fine. They don't have to be first-rate. The Ghost though is not British, but should be whatever natural voice comes from the actress. And the same is true with Mrs. Cratchit. When I heard my wonderful, talented friend Kristine Nielsen read the part, I didn't want to lose her own American rhythms or sound … so we let her (and subsequent Mrs. Cratchits) just use their own voices. And in ACT TWO, she expresses confusion as to why everyone else sounds British.

Silent Night. The way everybody sings that song so slowly drives me mad … it's like being stuck on a very slow-moving train. So usually it's quite an audience favorite when Bob Cratchit urges his children to sing slowly. However, find a balance — if it's so slow we actually are tortured, we won't find it funny anymore. So when they start it should be somewhat slow; when he slows them down, it should be too slow … but look for the balance where it's funny. At City Theatre we encouraged the wonderful Doug Rees as Scrooge to squirm and move around uncomfortably, in a big way, so that the audience had something to balance just the listening to the too-slow song. But beware of being too slow.

George Bailey and Clarence the angel are from the movie *It's a Wonderful Life*. Most people know that, but I thought I'd just spell it out in case you've never seen that film. (It's a pretty good film.)

ACT TWO bartender. If you want to do the play with one less person, the only stray problem is the ACT TWO bartender. If you're non-Equity, you can maybe use your stage manager for the part, or just some other person who wants a walk-on. Or if you're Equity, you can have one of the Cratchit actors double in the part — but because Mrs. Bob has just left the Cratchit family, I don't love the idea of seeing the Cratchits again, even subliminally. But if you gave one of them a really heavy moustache or something, it might work okay.

In the last scene Mrs. Bob and Scrooge turn into Leona and Harry (which most people know as Leona and Harry Helmsley). I do fear that for those people who don't know the Helmsleys, it may confuse. Leona was famous for being mean, as the head of all of Harry's hotels. There was a TV movie starring Suzanne Pleshette called *The Queen of Mean*. And she was also famous for tax evasion, and for saying "only the little people pay taxes." I find them useful for my purposes, but I hope if people don't know them, then their "type" will at least communicate.

I hope you have fun with it.

—Christopher Durang
January 2005